HALFSTONE

A TALE OF THE NARATHLANDS

Daniel White

Edited by Patricia Murphy and David Calver
Cover design by Ihor Tureha

For you.

CONTENTS

ACKNOWLEDGEMENTS

A very special thanks to Sam Blood, Jill Fernandes, and
Jordan Powell.

1

AN UNWELCOME ENCOUNTER

A few lingering strands of sunlight caught the evening mist. The remainder of the clearing was shrouded by the enclosing forest. It had always been a favourite location for Aldrick and his brother, Kaal, to visit while they were hunting. Often hungry rabbits and boar would forage among the brambles and tussocks that scattered the ground within. Today Aldrick was alone, as Kaal had remained behind to help their father, Braem, herd sheep on the farm. Equipped with a modestly crafted bow and a small number of arrows, Aldrick had left the house intent on scouting the weatherworn peaks of the Mountains Rain. These served as a colossal backdrop to the farm, which stretched down the lower, more fertile slopes of the mountains and beheld the tender coastline of the Remnan Ocean. It was a lengthy venture to the peaks and upon realising the time of day, Aldrick had wagered that he would not make it there and back again before nightfall. Instead, he chose to visit the clearing as it was no more than a half-hour walk away, nestled in the bowl of a small glacier-carved gully. As the falcon flies it was very close, but a vast cliff face blocked immediate passage to that part of the forest. The quickest way to reach it was to walk south through wheat fields, cross a wooden bridge that led into the forest, then follow a thin path that traced the rim of the cliff into the mountains, passing close by where the clearing hid.

Aldrick was standing at the edge of the clearing which, until this day, had felt all too familiar. At present he was frozen to the spot, unable to move. Something that had never been there before, that he had never laid eyes on, stood ahead of him—a deathly shadow through the mist. The beast was immense in comparison with any animal he was familiar with. It towered upon four great legs at a height clear of twice his own and besieged a ground space of no fewer than ten huddled stags. Although bulky, its body was sleek and catlike. Deep black hair composed its entire figure. From within, two narrowed eyes simmered orange. These were both fixed on him. The only movement in the entire clearing was the occasional wisp of condensed air from the beast's nostrils as it breathed in timely intervals. It was calm, composed. Aldrick was not. He knew exactly what it was. It was a ka-zchen—an ancient creature of prey, indigenous to the plains of the distant northern lands. Though they had once roamed wild, many were broken into servitude and used to slay their masters' adversaries. They were coined 'dark assassins' as they would dispatch their prey in swift and ruthless attacks beneath the blanket of night. Aldrick had learnt all this from Braem when he was a child, ever eager to hear the thrilling tales of the Narathlands.

His breath was stolen, not from sheer terror alone, but from the wonder of witnessing such an infamous, now mythical, killing creature. Why was it here in this forest he knew so well? His mind began to race. What if it was hunting him? What could he do if it attacked? If it did he would surely make easy prey. His heart throbbed savagely against his congested chest. This was a profoundly grim situation. He could run, but how would he possibly lose it if it pursued? There was no doubting that it would. Maybe he could seek shelter—climb a tree. He wanted to search for a nearby footing but feared that taking his eyes off the beast's own might provoke an attack.

Amidst the shock and fear he remembered his bow was in his hands, an arrow resting loosely on its grip. An attack was his best option. Not to try and kill the ka-zchen, for he would surely fail, but simply to distract it and buy him a few more crucial seconds to flee.

He needed to gather himself. His shot must be swift and the aiming precise enough to stall any immediate counter attack. There was no room for fault. The many hours Braem had spent teaching him how to handle his bow would now be put to the test.

"Be calm," he told himself.

The knowledge that he was alone, armed only with

the bow, was taunting his confidence. Like the sweat upon his brow he felt the moments slipping away. It wouldn't be long before the beast was upon him. His only chance was now. He took a breath and then in one, fluid movement, lifted the bow and drew the arrow. With the steel tip aimed between the beast's fiery eyes he released the arrow, turned and bolted. He heard a roar and then the thudding of paws as it came after him. Branches snapped against his body. The ground was unearthed beneath his feet. His bow and cloak were lost behind him as he fled from death. Through the trees he sped, the beast in close pursuit. Panic clotted his mind. He was thinking only of safety, of preservation. He was struck by the painful realisation that he could not find this at home. He could not lead the ka-zchen to his family! If it was he the beast was hunting then it was he who was burdened to see an end to its terror.

Stumbling back upon the forest path, Aldrick reached down and seized the fallen branch of a dying tree, then wheeled around. The ka-zchen was seconds from him. It pounced. With all his might he swung the branch, striking the side of the beast's head and one of its outstretched claws. The distracted animal's hulking shoulder smashed into his chest and he was thrust backwards, toward the cliff edge. In a desperate attempt to avoid falling to his doom he snatched at the air for something, anything, to grab hold of, but found nothing. This was it. This was the end. He began to fall, the ka-zchen toppling over him. In this instant he jolted to a sudden stop. Hanging down from the edge of the cliff were some protruding tree roots. Luckily, his arm had found its way into a mesh of them and his shoulder had caught his weight. He was saved. The ka-zchen, less fortunate, plummeted toward the ground. Its huge, helpless body struck rocks beside the streambed and it was no more.

Aldrick's body ached. His heart burst with every beat. He was suspended just below the top of the cliff with all of him, save for his lucky arm, dangling toward the ground. A searing pain erupted in his shoulder. The speed at which it caught the roots had dealt him damage. One dull predicament had led him here to the next. He had no strength left in him to climb back to level ground. Instead, he hung in pain, squinting down at his home far below. He wanted to call out, but the impact of the ka-zchen's body had knocked the wind from his own. For the moment he could do nothing but pray that the tree roots supporting him would not give way. He let his body relax. Perhaps, he thought, in time his family would come looking for him, although in reality he knew there was little chance they would set eyes on the cliff. From the house he must look no bigger than an ant where he hung, and with the fading light it was doubtful that he would be distinguishable against the rough and shaded stone. He was on his own.

The burden of his weight began to take its toll. From a short distance above him came the muffled snapping sound one hears when pulling plant from earth. He felt himself dip a small distance. Soon the roots would give way entirely and fate him to share the ka-zchen's misfortune.

"No!" he cried defiantly. He would not perish after surviving those past moments, after having witnessed the most remarkable and unearthly thing to occupy these lands in recent memory, after having survived it. He had to find a way back to secure ground. He had to get back atop the ridge. He would not die now!

Currents of wind began sweeping up the cliff face, swaying his body where he hung. Let it guide my hand, he thought. He reached up and grasped at whatever he could. Soon his body was turned, facing the sky, the trees. He was closer now, the wind his ethereal guide from below. While he climbed his shoulder throbbed, but he would not give in... almost there. One hand found grass and leaf. With a great heave the top half of his body resurfaced. His legs followed. He sprawled his spent body upon the ground and lay there, gasping for breath. His mind flickered with images of what had just happened. He recalled first seeing the ka-zchen, then fleeing from it. Falling, climbing... salvation. He was alive. He was here. The ka-zchen was not; it lay dead below him. It was over now. He could relax.

Aldrick remained upon the ground for some time, staring blankly upward. Wind gently rustled through the canopy as dusk seized the day. Regaining some sense of clarity, he pushed himself to his feet and, with his left arm supporting his right, made his way slowly down the path. In the failing light it was difficult to follow, but a familiarity with it and an unhurried pace made his step true. He had time. So long as he was home soon his family would not worry for him, though the story he was to tell would bring more than his own restless night in the household.

He had crossed the bridge and was making his way through the last wheat field before the house. It stood a modest dwelling, but it was spacious and sturdy. The walls were built of thick boulders, shaped to fit neatly together and conserve interior heat. In winter, due to the alpine altitude, these were required more than for the houses in the coastal village Rain, a short way to the south. The roofing remained of a likeness— thatched with burly wooden beams for support. For more than twenty years the house had stood strong, never once failing to provide ample shelter for his family.

As Aldrick approached, soft orange firelight met him through a gap between curtains. It was a greater comfort than ever before. He was home. For a moment he stood at the doorstep, beneath the eminent stars. He was blessed to be here in this place—with the warmth of a loving family and a sustainable home at hand. He lifted the latch and entered.

He was welcomed by the sounds and smell of a sumptuous dinner in preparation. Ahead of him, a lively fire crackled on the hearth and shed light to all corners of the living room. By it sat Braem and little Bree. They were in the midst of a playful quarrel. It appeared Bree had hidden something from Braem and was pressing him to guess its location. Aldrick smiled.

Braem looked up at him. "Ah, Aldrick, returning in time for a meal I see. Perhaps, if luck was with you,

you return with tomorrows?"

"Hello father," he replied with a wearied voice.

Braem stood, attention falling upon his battered appearance. "You're hurt." He came and showed Aldrick to the fireside. "Seat yourself."

Seeing his state, Bree abruptly lost her playful mood.

"Aldrick," she squeaked, eyes fixed upon him with fear and concern. "Aldrick, what is wrong with you?"

"Bree, go fetch your mother will you, and bring your brother some water. Now please." She hastily ran from the room. Braem found a seat and surveyed Aldrick with calm concern. "Aldrick, what happened out there? You look a mess."

"I am mostly all right," he replied. "I encountered something in the forest that would easily have finished me had it not been for fortunate circumstances." This was the truth; it was not skill that had spared his life. He had not intended to lead the ka-zchen off the cliff. He had simply ended up in the right place in the right moment.

"Tell me this wasn't the work of a boar runt," Braem said, forcing a chuckle, "I know they can be a pain." He frowned. "You are always careful, though. Your state eludes me."

"The cause of it will elude you further."

Bree returned with Phelvara and Kaal close behind her. She handed Aldrick a mug of cool water before making way for their mother to assess him. Kaal looked on, also allowing her to speak first.

"Aldrick, oh Aldrick, what is this?!" Phelvara

exclaimed in her motherly, overly fretful voice. She stooped and clutched Aldrick's good shoulder tightly, surveying his state. "Are you all right?!"

"Yes, I'm fine. You needn't worry." He glanced around at them all. "I have something to tell you, though." He hesitated, knowing well that he was about to incite alarm and quite possibly panic. "It was a ka-zchen."

There was a deathly silence. No one moved but Bree. She huddled behind her mother, sensing something was wrong.

"Go to your room, darling," Phelvara ordered.

Bree grasped her hand. "No, I won't!"

"It was in that clearing in the forest," Aldrick continued, gesturing in the general direction with his free hand. "It was huge. I didn't really know what to do. I tried to distract it with an arrow, then ran. It came at me by the cliff. I managed to hit it with a branch, but it knocked into me and we both went over the edge. Luckily, I got caught up in some tree roots." He felt his heart begin to race again as he relived those moments.

Phelvara turned to Braem. "Braem, a ka-zchen?! No!" Her voice was shrill. She was in disbelief, hysterics.

Braem looked at her and then back to Aldrick. There was fear in his eyes. It was a rare sight.

"You are very sure it was a ka-zchen?" he asked.

Aldrick nodded. "I am."

Braem rested an elbow on the table and stared into the flickering fire. "This is... bad."

Kaal now spoke. "A ka-zchen? Like in the old

stories? Aren't they all dead? No one has seen one in years… not here. Aldrick must be wrong."

"I didn't throw myself off the cliff for no reason," he retorted, annoyed. His brother was often doubtful of his words.

Kaal didn't reply, just continued to eye him sceptically.

"Aldrick, you said it fell down the cliff, yes?" asked Braem. "I am hoping you saw it die. We cannot have it prowling here." He spoke with containment, his fear subdued by reason.

"Yes, it fell. It landed by the stream. I didn't see it moving. From that height I assumed it must have been killed." Doubt crept into Aldrick's mind. Was it dead? Had he too hastily dismissed a threat that might return to haunt them? "We have to check!" he exclaimed.

"Yes, we must," agreed Braem. "But you must stay here. Vara will see you are cared for. Kaal and I will go."

"Braem, no. It's too dark now. Wait for the morning, won't you?" pleaded Phelvara. She clutched a terrified Bree in her arms.

Braem looked at her gravely. "This cannot wait, Vara. We have to be sure." He turned to Kaal. "Come."

They readied themselves quickly. They lit torches from the flames of the fire, armed themselves with bows and hunting knives from a cabinet by the door, then left into the night. Phelvara told Bree to mind the cooking, then tenderly ushered Aldrick to his room. He felt blissful comfort as he collapsed upon his bed. After seeing he was resting, Phelvara left to heat water for his injuries.

Now alone, Aldrick found his mind flooded with questions and concern. Was the ka-zchen dead? Where had it come from? Why had it come here? He turned onto his back and rubbed his eyes, ill at ease.

When Phelvara returned she sat by him and wiped his face with a warm cloth, cleaning scratches he had received as he fled through the forest, then gave him a soothing ointment made from garden herbs to rub into his inflamed shoulder. She had always been an exceptionally caring parent, pausing whatever she was doing to make sure her family was well and content. Yet while she tended to him now, her face was a deathly white. He had received far worse injuries as a child, but the fact that these ones were the result of an encounter with a ka-zchen was visibly causing her much anxiety.

"I just can't believe this has happened," she said, leaving his side and walking to the window.

"It's all right, Mother. I am sure the ka-zchen is dead now," he said as confidently as he dared. "It probably wandered down here from the north. I strayed upon it by chance."

He hoped it had just been chance, yet he couldn't shake the thought that the beast had been lurking there for a reason. Why else had it been troubled enough to enter a crowded forest that constricted its passage? This had been the reason it did not easily catch up to him while he fled—it had found sprinting between the trees more trying than he.

Phelvara left the window and made to exit. "I'm

going to check upon Bree and wait for the others. You stay and rest. We will eat later."

He wanted to wait with her. He feared for Braem and Kaal and needed to know that they were safe, that the ka-zchen had indeed perished. Not only that, but he wanted the reassurance of knowing they had witnessed the beast with their own eyes and did not doubt his far-fetched and nightmarish tale of encountering it. Phelvara's instructions to remain put were wise, however. He was in no state to leave. He made himself comfortable and closed his eyes.

Aldrick heard the front door open and close, then voices. Braem and Kaal had returned. Phelvara was with them in the living room. Feeling a sudden spurt of energy, he pushed himself to his feet and made his way to them. They stood together by the fireside, talking in hushed voices but grave tones. Bree was watching them with one eye from behind her door.

"Was it there?" he asked nervously.

They turned to him.

"Yes, it was," replied Kaal, looking rather daunted. "It's dead."

He felt relief sweep through him. He nodded. "Good."

Braem and Phelvara continued to stare at him, their faces both pale. Something was wrong.

"What?" he asked anxiously.

"Aldrick," Braem began. "I don't believe the ka-zchen was here by chance… it had been branded with the sign of a master on its chest."

His heart leapt. "It... had a master? What was the sign?"

"A blue butterfly."

"A blue butterfly," he repeated. "Blue? But brands aren't coloured. Do you mean it was inked on?"

"No, it had been branded... with magic."

2

SUN AND RAIN

When Aldrick opened his eyes in the morning it was as if he had woken into a dream. Usually his first thoughts were of the long day of work that lay ahead of him, either helping Braem on the farm or hunting in the forest. Today though, he found his mind occupied by giant beasts, magic and unsolved mysteries. Excitement brimmed within him. There was a dull ache in his shoulder but it would not impede him. He had to get up and go to where the ka-zchen lay. He had to see it—confirm the world in which he lived really was one of fantasy, that all those childhood stories were true. He sprang upright, threw on some worn trousers and a cotton shirt, then made his way through the house whilst still buttoning it. At the door he jumped into his boots, socks absent, and ran outside, oblivious to his slapdash appearance.

It was a fine day. The view was stunning but

presently he had little interest in sightseeing. He made straight for the base of the cliff. Dew had settled over the farm in the night and his trousers were dampened to the thighs as he made his way through the fields. It didn't bother him. He scrambled over one last wooden fence and up a small rise from where he could look down upon the stream.

There it was—a black mound upon the rocks. Kaal stood by it. Aldrick made his way down to him and stopped at his side. Neither of them spoke a word, only staring in awe. Up close, the ka-zchen was even more terrifying than he remembered. It was huge. Though now limp and lifeless, razor-sharp claws remained fully extended from its padded feet. Its head lay on one side, the rocks around it stained by black blood. He had at first likened the beast's sleek body to that of a cat, but now saw that the head shared similarities with a wolf's. It was elongated with flared nostrils at its snout. Its mouth hung open on a slant revealing huge, jagged fangs rooted in strong jaws. Its ears were stiff and pointed at the tips. Below them, wide eyes hid behind tufts of black hair. Their orange flare had faded and they were now a vacant grey. It smelt foul—like an aged, damp dog, only twice as potent.

After some time Kaal broke their silence. "It's... big," he murmured.

Aldrick nodded, not taking his eyes off it.

Throughout their lives, he and Kaal had done much together. They were very close. But surviving the ka-zchen was something Aldrick had achieved on his own. Although his mind was unspoken, Aldrick knew

Kaal was impressed by this. He in turn was quietly thankful. This moment they shared together now, awestruck by the deathly sight before them.

There was more than the appearance of the ka-zchen on Aldrick's mind, however. He wanted answers to lingering questions—who had sent it and why? Braem and Phelvara had acted oddly last night, blindly refusing to offer any insight beyond the magical nature of the brand... the brand! Suddenly remembering this, Aldrick stepped closer to look for it. It wasn't hard to find. Near the centre of the beast's chest was a small area where its hair was shaven. On the exposed skin was a dark blue butterfly outlined in gold. Magic had made this! It was unlike any marking Aldrick had seen before. It appeared as a coloured tattoo, only the colouring was uncanny; it was brilliantly rich and glinted ever so slightly, almost like the powder on the wings of a real butterfly. It was as if the brand had appeared there without the craft of any tool. Could it really be that a wizard wished him dead? The thought was crazy.

Kaal's eyes were on him. "You know, last night that brand was the first thing Father looked for when we came here. He didn't even stop to make sure the beast was dead, just went straight to that, like he expected it to have a master." Kaal hesitated briefly, then continued. "And he said something to me, Aldrick... he said they have found you."

Aldrick stared at him.

"They?" he repeated to himself. "This is crazy. What would anyone want with me? I'm kind of, well, ordinary and boring, aren't I?"

"I thought so," replied Kaal jokingly, then his tone became serious once more. "I was thinking—maybe it has something to do with your past, with your parents or something."

"My parents?" Aldrick was taken aback. "My parents are here." He knew well that Braem and Phelvara had taken him in as an infant, but this was fairly common in these parts. People were kind and supportive and very few orphaned children remained so for long. He rarely mused on his lineage. Ever since he could remember he had been a son to the Fletchers.

"Yes, I know—we are your family," said Kaal politely. "But it's worth considering, right? I mean, can you think of a better explanation for why something like this," he gestured toward the ka-zchen, "would find itself at our doorstep?"

Aldrick couldn't. They were a simple, good-faring family who lived away from the busyness and troubles of the surrounding world. If what Kaal suggested was true, he found no sense in it.

"Surely my real parents were also ordinary and boring. Why would someone who had a quarrel with them want me dead all these years later?" Though sceptical, he couldn't deny that some part of him was warming to the idea that his origin story might bear some unspoken significance. He had no desire to be hunted, but the thought that he was somehow entwined with a world where magic existed was enticing.

Kaal shrugged.

"Time will tell us all," he said. "Perhaps Father was wrong and it was simply a stray and you happened to meet it up there." He peered up the cliff. "Hell, that's a long fall."

"Most likely," Aldrick said, also looking up. "Even if it did have a master, it wasn't necessarily under orders when I came across it, right? It probably came at me because I made it mad—shooting at it... looks like I managed to completely miss."

Kaal frowned. "Still, I wonder who its master is. We should ask Father today. Hopefully he'll be more eager to talk than he was last night."

Aldrick nodded. "We'll get the whole story. There has to be some half-reasonable explanation for all this."

"There always is."

They left the ka-zchen's rocky grave. No longer in a hurry, Aldrick took time to acknowledge the beauty the morning had brought to the land. Everything looked fresh and awake. The air smelt of damp earth and grass. In the heights of the forest, moss birds sang their gentle songs in union. A few wisps of mist lingered in the sky but did not block the sun's light from greeting the lower coastal land. Every field, brush and knoll between them and the ocean flaunted the tepid colours of autumn. The ocean itself was a restful turquoise. Behind the house Phelvara was throwing breadcrumbs to enthusiastic sparrows, and out the front Bree rode around on a pretend pony that Braem had fashioned for her from a lancewood stick and an old straw pillow. Braem was probably down in a lower field herding sheep to fresh pasture. Everything was as it should be, save for the creature's corpse behind them. It remained out of place in some ineffably strange and ominous way. Perhaps it was the magic it bore with it. Aldrick considered this until Kaal interrupted his thoughts.

"Do you want to come with me to Rain today?" he asked. "I'm taking the cart. We need to sell some things at the market. You could just relax and enjoy the ride. I'm sure you are fit for it."

"I'll come along," said Aldrick. A trip to the village would be nice. He feared that if he stayed Phelvara would insist he remain indoors under her over-nurturing watch. Suddenly he remembered something and stopped walking. "When do you plan on leaving?"

"Soon, I want to be there by noon."

"All right, but first let me fetch some things I dropped in the forest yesterday. As you might imagine, I was in quite a hurry."

Kaal chuckled. "I'm sure you were," he said. "I'll ready the horses and see you back here soon." He continued on.

"See you." Aldrick changed his course and made his way across the bridge and up into the forest. He found it to be once more its calm, peaceful self. Only moss birds and the odd few little mammals lingered within the trees. His possessions were easily retrievable. The ka-zchen had kindly made a clear pathway through the undergrowth while chasing him and he could now follow it back toward the clearing and pick them up as he went. For a moment he considered that they may be able to track where the ka-zchen had come from, but concluded that it would be a foolish endeavour. Its prints would undoubtedly lead far beyond the forest and eventually fade from the earth. He still sought answers, though. Who was its master and why had it been sent here? He would ask Braem all of this in the evening after returning from Rain. Bothering Phelvara about it now would not be wise.

Before leaving for Rain, Aldrick had a hasty breakfast and dressed in some more presentable clothes—fine cloth pants and a tunic. He chose to wear sandals as he wasn't wearing socks anyway. Kaal wore similar clothes but had chosen a dyed black leather vest. Aldrick had noticed his brother always wore black to the village and guessed this was because he thought it attracted the women folk. Admittedly, Kaal was always two steps ahead of him when it came to courting women. It must be his clothing.

After Aldrick had successfully avoided Phelvara and said goodbye to Bree, the two of them set off down their road. It took a little time to reach the base of the mountains. The road wound its way back and forth down the slope to reduce its steepness, and there were half a dozen gates to be opened along the way. However, at level ground it met the coastal road between Farguard and Rain and they were free to be on their way. Aldrick sat on the back of the cart, accompanied by some sacks of grain, garden vegetables, and salted meats that were to be sold at the market. The journey felt brief. It was filled with hearty chatter and accompanied by a refreshing sea breeze.

Shortly before noon, they found themselves at the entrance to Rain. It was a large village. Being the main port in the south meant that business prospered and many people from the province and neighbouring lands sought to earn their livings here. The streets were well kept and the people kept well. Democracy reigned and social progress was promoted. The appearance of the various dwellings reflected this with every one suggesting a fair income and many a door being left open wide and welcoming. Occasionally one would hear news of a tavern brawl or a petty theft, but this was generally caused by newcomers who were soon to learn that incivility was not lightly dismissed.

At the centre of the village, a little way in from the docks, was a large market ground that was always busy on a fine day. He and Kaal made their way there through the crowded streets. They found the market to be particularly lively. Music and dance was abundant. People's spirits were high. They were making the most of the last warm days of autumn.

When they had found a free stand and unhitched the cart, Kaal led their horses to stables and left Aldrick to mind the produce. He was glad to do so. Being around people always raised him up. He often felt isolated on their farm and village trips were a welcome escape.

When Kaal returned he decided that because Aldrick was in such a good mood, he could handle business himself and left again to join in the dancing, most likely in the hopes of meeting a fine young lady or two. Aldrick was a little jealous, but happy to exchange cheerful banter with customers as they made their market rounds. Trade flourished and in short time there was but one sack of Phelvara's greenstone beans left to be sold. No one seemed to want them.

Just as Aldrick was considering returning the beans to the cart, a hooded figure approached from within the milling crowd. It paused in front of the stand and stood staring down at it, face concealed.

"Afternoon, can I help you?" he inquired politely. There was no response. "Only the beans left to buy I'm afraid," he continued. "They are actually very nice... if you boil them for long enough."

Now the figure spoke. "Yes, I will have them." It was a raspy female voice. She sounded northern, perhaps even from as far as the Greater Northern Provinces.

"The beans it is, then. That will be three in bronze, thanks."

She handed him two silver coins from a leather pouch at her side.

He grinned. "I'll give you your change if I may see whom I serve. You're not from around here, are you?"

She hesitated for a moment then slowly, cautiously, removed her hood. A flood of hair fell to her waist as she lifted her head, smiling at him. He felt a flutter as his heart was stolen. He was gazing upon a young woman, no more than a year older than himself, who bore all the beauty and grace in the world upon her face. She was perfect, too much so to be real. Her skin was a fine ochre silk; her cheeks smooth and rounded, as impeccably curved as the contours of the moon. Her eyes were the lucid green of a rainforest, accentuated by those waterfalls of ebony locks. She was a beauty beyond words, beyond belief.

"No. I am from Daraki' Anya," she replied.

"Daraki' Anya..." he repeated mindlessly. "That's nice. Is it... nice there?"

"It can be, though I have not been there in some time now."

"Well, I am glad you are here now to buy some beans," he said, handing her change. "I'm Aldrick by the way."

"I'm Télia."

"It is nice to meet you, Télia." He offered her his hand. She took it. Hers was warm and soft, like her gaze.

"It is lovely to meet you too, Aldrick," she said.

A silence followed her words in which he couldn't help but stare at her with what no doubt appeared a gawky grin on his face.

"I think shaking hands is a strange tradition," she continued, letting his hand go. "In Daraki we always greet strangers with a hug. You can tell a lot about a character from the way they hug."

"We can do that if you like," he said hopefully.

"Very well."

They met beside the stand and embraced one another. What was left of Aldrick's heart melted. Télia's body was warm. Her head reached only to his chin and her hair smelt like a meadow of blossoming wildflowers. He had no desire to ever let go, but eventually they parted. Another silence ensued. Before it became awkward he made to break it.

"So what did that hug tell you about me?" he asked.

"That you are a kind and tender person, Aldrick," she said, looking deep into his eyes. "Did it tell you something about me?"

He thought for a moment. "I think it did, but I'm not sure exactly what... perhaps that you are the same."

She shrugged. "Perhaps... or perhaps I am horrible."

He laughed. "I doubt that."

"You mustn't judge strangers too hastily, Aldrick," she advised. Her eyes flitted across the crowd. "I should go now, but I will be close, you know. You live nearby, I presume?" She returned her hood to her head.

"Yes, I do—on a farm just a little way north of here against the Mountains Rain."

"Ahh." She nodded thoughtfully. "Well, I am certain our paths shall cross again very soon. Farewell for now, Aldrick." She turned on her heel and left, carrying the last basket of beans and all that was beautiful in the world away with her.

"Farewell," he said after her. He wanted her to stay. Never had such a brief encounter with a woman made him feel so giddy, so childlike. He had half a mind to go after her, but what would he say to her? The moment had passed. The only cloud in the sky drifted in front of the sun.

Kaal returned. He had seen Télia leaving.

"Aldrick is in love with a mystery woman," he teased, slapping him firmly on the back.

"Whatever you say, Brother," was all Aldrick found as a retort. He knew he wouldn't be able to convincingly deny it.

Kaal frowned in the direction Télia had left. "I wonder why she wears that hood... maybe she's a thief, Aldrick. Maybe your coins are missing..."

He didn't bother checking. She was too fair to be such, and even if she was, he would let her steal from him as often as she pleased. His mind wandered.

Kaal looked down at the empty stand. "Everything sold I see."

"Yes, all gone. It was a good day."

"Let's head home then. I'll fetch the horses."

After hitching the horses to the cart, they bought some chocolate muffins to eat and were on their way. Aldrick peered back as they left the bustling crowds, hoping to catch a glimpse of Télia. She was nowhere to be seen. Perhaps that had been the only time their paths would ever cross, and she had suggested otherwise out of sheer politeness. He hoped not. He thought of her outlandish beauty. How green her eyes were. Did many people from Daraki' Anya share that feature, or was it hers alone? He liked to think it was the latter. He cared not for the thought of anyone else. Those short moments they had shared together, he was thankful for.

The ride home was enjoyable. The sun had returned and drenched the countryside in golden light. Rabbits hopped about in the fields and birds chirped cheerfully within the blackberry vines that entangled fencing at either side of the road. Far to the north, the peaks of the Midland Ranges were visible, a soft blue in the distance. Aldrick and Kaal's spirits soared and they shared stories and songs and spoke of travel and adventure, of their hopes and aspirations. Aldrick had always wanted to travel far away from here someday. Often he imagined what the rest of the Narathlands might be like. From the tales he had heard it sounded as though there were many places to be explored, many sights to be seen and many secrets to be discovered. Thinking of such things brought the events of last night back to the forefront of his mind. He remembered his plan to question Braem about the ka-zchen. Who was its magic-bearing master? Could it truly be that its appearance was linked to the faded truth that he had been an orphan? As they ascended their winding road these thoughts drowned out all else. Anticipation rose within. He wanted the truth.

At the top of the road they unhitched the cart from the horses, led them to the shade of the stables and generously fed and watered them. They then proceeded into the house to find it cool and quiet. The rest of the family were still outdoors. Aldrick was willing to be patient. His questions could wait until the evening. Besides, there was much to be done in the meantime. Fences needed mending, tracks needed maintenance, wood needed cutting and arrows needed crafting. He chose to make arrows as it was the job that would stress his shoulder the least. Although it was a fairly simple task, given the parts were purchased in bulk from a trader in Rain, he enjoyed crafting each arrow with loving attention, particularly when it came to fletching. By carefully trimming the pheasant feathers, the accuracy of a long-distance shot was increased by a significant amount.

The sun was setting when Aldrick finished. He had crafted twenty-three arrows, claiming ten for his own quiver. The encounter with the ka-zchen had inspired him to put more time and effort into archery. Braem had made a target for him and Kaal to practice on a few years earlier which he planned to put to good use. He seldom hit the centre mark.

Aldrick heard Phelvara and Bree making their way inside through the back door and went to them. "Hello you two, how did the day treat you?"

Phelvara smiled at him. "Well, thank you. We have been very busy." She began to help Bree take off a dress which had been dirtied in the garden. "How was the market? Did you fair well?"

"Yes, we should have coin enough for the month."

"Lovely, though we ought to be saving for the winter now."

"That's a good idea... you don't happen to know where Braem is, do you?" he asked.

Phelvara did not reply immediately. The brightness in her face drained away. She appeared wary— reluctant to speak. The expression reminded Aldrick of the state she had been in for much of last night after learning of the ka-zchen's brand.

"Your father is away for a few days, visiting Jon," she said finally, avoiding Aldrick's eye.

This came as a surprise. Jon was an old family friend who had not visited the farm for a number of years now. He resided deep in the Midland Ranges, far more isolated than they were here. Aldrick held many fond memories of Jon. He had once visited regularly, bringing with him enthralling news and tales even more wondrous than Braem's. Many were difficult to believe. Indeed, they made everyday life feel rather mundane. It was odd that Braem would travel so far to see the old man after such a long period without sharing words.

"He's gone to Jon's? Why?"

Phelvara shrugged. "He was just a little concerned about that ka-zchen, that's all. He thinks Jon will know more about it." She glanced up at him with a forced smile that offered little reassurance.

"About it or about who sent it?" he asked pressingly, hoping for a more elaborate explanation. It was a mistake.

Phelvara sighed irritably. "Ask no more of it. If there is something to know Braem will bring the news when he returns. Until then let us forget all about that ghastly beast. It's dead."

He let it go, but knew there was more to this story. Phelvara would not have let Braem travel so far on such short notice unless it had been very important, and what insights could Jon offer? As far as he remembered, Jon wasn't someone whom his parents considered a guiding figure. Braem had often referred to him as a 'wild old dog'.

Again Aldrick was left to mull over such things in

his own head. He sensed things were in the process of changing somehow. For better or for worse, he did not know. Only time would tell.

When he fell asleep that night he was met by dreams not of the ka-zchen or the enveloping mystery, but of the astonishingly beautiful woman he had met at the market that day. Télia was her name. Télia.

3

THE WIELDER'S AERA

It was near closing time. She sat at a small table as close as possible to the open fire. Cold and loneliness harried her. She was irritable. She didn't want to be here. Had she been in Galdrem at the time the contract became available they might have hired someone with more experience, someone who knew these parts. It was solely because she happened to be nearby that she was assigned the job. Having to be so far from home wasn't what annoyed her though. In fact, she loved travel, but this time the details were given to her on too short notice and had been exceptionally vague: 'Make haste to Rain and be aera to the young wielder Aedimon. Reinforcements to follow'. Supposedly this wielder was in imminent danger.

Rain had proved to be a busy place and she had found no one of, nor anyone who knew of the name Aedimon in the village. It hadn't been until today that she had sensed the close presence of a wielder, a very powerful one. In the market place he had been—a young man, near her age. His name was Aldrick. He had appeared to be completely unaware of the fact he was a wielder at all. It was a curious thing. Never had she met one so oblivious to it. In the north, wielders were proud and often arrogant, but Aldrick... he was nice, kind hearted. It had been a breath of fresh air and she felt rather inclined to keep knowledge of his powers from him, at least for the time being. There was little doubt in her mind that he was the wielder she was assigned to protect; he just wasn't known locally by the name Aedimon. The chance of there being another young wielder this far south was decidedly slim. Outside of the capital province they were few and far between.

While talking with him she had noticed that he sported an injury, and more alarmingly, he had the faint scent of ka-zchen upon him. After learning from him where he lived, she had hastily bought a map of the province and found the exact location of his farm. It was important she venture there tonight. She must ensure the ka-zchen posed no ongoing threat and discover who its master was. If she knew the enemy, she could hunt them. With any luck the reinforcements would find her soon. They were likely pitted against a very dangerous adversary.

When the last few patrons had left the tavern, Télia went upstairs to her room. She put on her coat and cloak, then equipped herself with her crossbow and a number of light daggers that she had stowed under the bed. Fortunately, her window was at the rear of the tavern just above the roof of the ground floor and was an ideal passage for one intending to exit in secret. She had been trained to take such precautions. An aera could never be too careful.

Once on the ground, she made her way from shadow to shadow to the stables where her horse awaited.

"Hello De'ama," she whispered softly. "We ride tonight."

De'ama shifted excitedly, but soundlessly. As an aera's horse she too had been taught to move with stealth when necessary. Télia led her down back streets all the way to the village gates before mounting. In the north, the full face of Solemn graced the sky, bathing the surrounding countryside in pale blue light. After glancing back to be sure they had not been followed, she patted De'ama gently on the neck and they were on their way.

In less than half an hour they arrived at the farm's entrance. She dismounted, offered De'ama words of comfort, then began to make her way up the slope. Because there were livestock in many of the lower fields that might stir in her presence, Télia stole toward the edge of the forest. Here, she found a rocky, dried-up stream bed that provided her with a sheltered path upwards. Soon enough she was nearing the farmhouse. She climbed out of the stream where she was able and peered around. A small bridge lay ahead of her that offered passage to the fields beside the house. She stopped and thought for a moment. She did not want to get too close and risk waking anyone inside, nor did she wish to leave evidence of her presence. So, she continued past the bridge and up the edge of an arching cliff which separated the farm from the mountain forest. Beneath a blanket of trees she found a suitable vantage point to examine the area below.

There was a foul whiff on the air—the scent of ka-zchen. One was very close. She readied her crossbow and lowered her figure to the ground. For a while she didn't move, only listened. The creature couldn't be in the forest, otherwise it would make noise. She looked down upon the farmhouse and surrounding fields. There was no movement there either. She was about to turn her gaze when she noticed fresh tracks in the field nearest her. They led her eyes to a black mound at the base of the cliff. It was the ka-zchen! It was... dead. She let out a small gasp. Dead? Maybe Aldrick was aware that he was a wielder after all; how else had it met such a fate? Eager to investigate the creature's corpse she made her way to it, treading with less caution than before.

Solemn's light made the animal's features easily distinguishable. She sought only to locate its brand. Soon enough a glint of blue caught her eye. It was a drathen butterfly. Fear stole her. This was far worse than she had anticipated. Aldrick was in grave danger!

"Don't move."

Télia was already more alarmed than she had been in a long time. The voice behind her did not heighten this. Accepting she was compromised, she calmly placed her crossbow on the ground, raised her hands and turned around. A tall young man with dark hair stood ahead of her, an armed bow ready in his hands. She recognised him.

"You're the girl from the market, aren't you?" he asked sharply.

"Yes I am. And you, you are Aldrick's brother?"

He hesitated for a moment. "Yes... tell me why you are here. Are you here for him? Did you send that thing to kill him?" He nodded toward the ka-zchen.

"Yes. Yes I am here for Aldrick. I am here to protect him. I did not send the ka-zchen."

He looked taken aback. "Protect him? From whom?"

"From someone very bad." She had not the time for this conversation. "Look, I must speak with your brother. Will you trust in me to meet with him in the morning? The hour is already late tonight."

He stepped closer.

"How do you know who hunts Aldrick? Tell me!" he demanded fiercely.

"The brand. I know from its brand," she hissed.

"Why do they want him dead?"

"Now is not the time. You and Aldrick will meet with me at the entrance to your farm at sunrise tomorrow," she stated bluntly.

Aldrick's brother looked irritated but his decision was wise.

"Very well," he said, lowering his bow and taking another step forward. "But know that if you bring harm to my family, I will have your life."

"You have my word." Télia picked her crossbow

back up. "Remember—tomorrow, at sunrise."

She left him standing there and made to retrace her steps down the streambed. Her mind was humming. Selayna? How was it possible? Hadn't she died many years ago? Télia knew now why it was so important she protect Aldrick, why reinforcements were being sent—word of Seleyna's return had reached Galdrem. The Synod was responsive to her manoeuvres. Why was Aldrick a target though? Télia thought hard upon this. The name Aedimon... it suddenly felt familiar. Why? No answers came to her. There were many pieces to this puzzle and she could not fit them together herself. She needed somewhere safe that she could take Aldrick and search for the answers they now both sought. She knew exactly where to go— where she had originally been going—to the wielder Jon's.

4
BE WARY OF THE SHADOWS

"Get up. Aldrick, get up."

It was still dark.

He groaned and squinted up at a flaming torch above his bed. Kaal was holding it. "What?"

"I said get up. We have an appointment with your lady friend."

He rubbed his eyes. "What are you talking about?"

"That girl from the market—she was here last night. She wants to speak with you. Get up."

"Télia." Aldrick stood immediately. "Where is she?" he asked, dressing hurriedly.

"We are meeting her down the hill at sunrise. Bring your bow."

"Kaal, she was here?"

"Yes, after midnight. I thought I heard something so I went out and found her by the ka-zchen. Aldrick, she knows who sent it."

Kaal proceeded to tell him everything Télia had said. He listened intently. How was she involved in all this? Maybe she could answer the many questions he had. Either way he was eager to speak with her again. Even just seeing her would make this a fine day.

The sun had yet to dawn when they reached the bottom of their road. There was a chill in the air and mist hung low. They waited anxiously on their side of the fence. Kaal's bow was armed. He feared Télia planned to ambush them. Aldrick dismissed this, but knew he ought to be watchful nonetheless. His bow was at his side.

While the sun's first light spilt over the horizon the sound of hooves grew louder upon the road to Rain. Télia appeared astride a beautiful black mare. She was hooded, as she had been yesterday at the market. Aldrick now supposed their encounter had been no coincidence.

"Hello again," she said, drawing to a halt at the opposite side of the fence.

He smiled. "Hello. I hear you want to speak with me?"

She returned the smile only briefly. She looked anxious. Kaal was keeping his distance, watching her through narrowed eyes.

"I am sure your brother has already told you much from last night?" she asked, glancing at him.

"He did. He said you know who hunts me?"

"I do. Her name is Selayna. She is a most wicked wielder."

"Wielder? What do you mean?"

"I mean that... well, I suppose I mean she is a witch."

"Witch..." Aldrick repeated under his breath. "Why does she want me dead?"

"That is a question to which I do not have an answer. What concerns me is that you may still be in danger. Aldrick, it is not safe for you here."

"Why is this your concern? Why do you want to protect me?"

"It is my duty."

"So you are a bodyguard?"

"Of sorts, yes." Télia's words were hurried. "Aldrick, I can take you to a safer place where someone more knowledgeable than I may be able to shed light on all this."

She wanted him to leave with her? It was a bold thought.

"Where is this place?" Aldrick asked curiously. "Who is this person?"

"Deep in the Midland Ranges. A trusted wielder resides there."

"What is his name...?"

"Jon."

He and Kaal stared at each other.

"Jon? Jon is our friend. He is no wielder," said Kaal self-assuredly.

Télia raised her eyebrows.

"You know him?" she asked. "Interesting... well, I can assure you with confidence—he is a wielder."

Kaal shook his head adamantly. "No, no he isn't! He is a harmless old man."

"Wielder!" insisted Télia. "They are out there you know, and much closer than you may think." She shot Aldrick a sly but unreadable glance.

His head was ready to explode. She wanted to take him to safety—protect him from some evil wielder who wished him dead. And Jon, Jon was also a wielder? Was that why Braem had left to see him? None of it made any sense.

"What if I just stayed here?" he asked, overwhelmed.

"Then you would eventually be hunted down and killed. More enemies will come, Aldrick. You must come with me now. It ensures the safety of your family too."

Télia's words were wise, he supposed. He wanted no harm to befall his family because of him, and he ached for answers to an ever-mounting number of questions. At Jon's he might finally have these.

He turned to Kaal. "I should go."

Kaal was fuming. "You want to leave with her? But none of this should be our problem! We can handle ourselves here and let people like her and Jon sort this out." He was searching for excuses.

"But I need to know the truth. I have to go!" Aldrick blurted.

"Aldrick, we must leave as soon as possible," Télia said with urgency. "I am ready. You should prepare yourself now. It will take us two days to reach the ranges and there may be danger along the way. Your family should seek shelter in Rain in the meantime. They will be safe there, though they should remain watchful. I recommend your brother stay with them."

He turned to Kaal and looked him over. "Will you stay with Bree and Phelvara until Braem returns?"

"I suppose I could do that," Kaal muttered reluctantly.

Aldrick looked back at Télia. "Well, I guess I'll go and prepare for the journey."

"Meet me here when you are ready, Aldrick," she said as he and Kaal made to leave. "Don't be long."

They walked back up their road in silence. All the while Aldrick could sense Kaal's ill mood. He probably wanted to leave with him, or perhaps he was just worried. He had every right to be.

When they entered the house they found Phelvara arisen and sipping tea in her gown by the embers of last night's fire. She looked up at them as they approached. "Hello boys, you are up early... is something wrong?" She had noticed the anxious expressions upon their faces.

Aldrick took her hand. "Mother, there is little time to explain. The ka-zchen was hunting me. There is a woman here to protect me. She says I will be safer at Jon's. I'm going to go there with her. You must leave here too, in case more danger comes. Will you move to Rain for a few days and await Braem's return? I know this is all crazy, but it is important that we all be careful." He took a breath.

She looked upon him in bewilderment. "Oh Aldrick, if you say this is the best thing then I have to believe you. We will go to Rain, as you ask. And you," she touched his cheek with a gentle hand, "you pursue the answers you rightfully seek."

It was a much better response than he had expected. He smiled. "Hopefully I won't be too long. Perhaps in a week I'll return. We'll see."

Aldrick prepared for the journey hurriedly. He felt lightheaded and a little sick. Life was changing rapidly and keeping pace with it was exhausting. Into a leather travelling bag he stuffed everything he would need: a change of clothes, a pillow and enough food to last him until Farguard. He already had his bow and wore hunting gear, but decided to add two knives to his belt and extra arrows to his quiver. He couldn't be too careful.

Outside, he saddled and then fastened his gear onto his favourite steed, Tame. The horse whinnied excitedly at the prospect of open travel and pranced merrily about in the morning sun once readied.

All that was left to do now was to say farewell to Phelvara and Kaal. Bree was still fast asleep inside and he would not wake her. Phelvara came and hugged him tightly. She had tears in her eyes and breathed in heavy gasps.

"Be calm. It's all going to be fine," he said softy, attempting to subdue her emotions.

She smiled and wiped the tears away.

"Yes it will be," she sniffled before fresh tears took their place. "Aldrick, I'm sorry Braem and I have raised you in such a sheltered lifestyle. There is much more for you out there than we can ever offer here. You are greater than you know."

Aldrick took her by the shoulders. "I love living

here, Mother. This place is always going to be home to me. You and Braem are the greatest parents, to all three of us. Don't worry about me out there. The woman I ride with is trustworthy. She wants the best for us all."

Phelvara cried more and they hugged for some time longer. When she finally let him go, Aldrick turned to Kaal. He stood nearby, resting his weight on his bow and watching Aldrick with an inscrutable expression.

"I'll see you, Brother," Aldrick said.

Kaal sighed, then came and thumped him on the shoulder. "Don't go getting yourself into any trouble. If a ka-zchen eats you I'll use that girlfriend of yours for target practice."

Aldrick laughed. "I'll be fine." He mounted Tame then looked back. "Goodbye! Tell Bree I say bye to her too, and that she should look after her mother!" He raised a hand and was on his way.

While Aldrick rode down the hill, fear and apprehension no longer hounded him. He was only anxious with excitement. He was going on a journey with a beautiful woman, a journey that would connect the life he knew to a world only spoken of in tales and wandered in dreams, one in which magic and mighty beasts still dwelled. Whatever else was there to discover in lands he had yet to lay eyes upon?

Télia awaited him at the gate, sitting gracefully upon her mare. She had removed her hood and her flurries of hair danced gently in the morning breeze.

"Are you ready?" she asked.

He glanced back at his home on the mountainside. "Yes, I am. We ride for Farguard?"

She nodded. "We need to make as much ground as possible under the sun. If there are more ka-zchen about they will stalk at night, in the shadows."

Aldrick took a breath. "Well then, I guess we should be on our way."

"Yes."

They began to ride. Télia led, galloping swiftly. He hoped Tame would be able to maintain her Mare's pace. The farm horses seldom journeyed at a speed beyond a trot and the road would be long. Presently, Tame appeared to be enjoying the freedom and held his own with ease.

The immediate road north Aldrick knew well for he and Kaal had roamed the surrounding fields and gullies as children, seeking out anything that captured their imaginations and playing games that entertained them while they avoided whatever chores Braem and Phelvara had set for them that day. It wasn't long before they had left these familiar places behind them, though, and made their way down a rocky crag into a vast, low-lying woodland valley that stretched far inland. The road to Farguard kept to the left, following closely to the white sand coastline. The trees shied away from its borders, but their branches reached far and clumps of slender leaves hung at head height around them. Grass covered the ground where it could; a deep green in the shade while bright and vibrant where the sun's light touched it. It was strange travelling through such a serene landscape when he knew such grave dangers lay ahead. Perhaps this was all a prolonged dream.

Very late in the afternoon, after only two brief stops to eat and rest the horses, they came upon a great opening in the woods through which a shallow river ran to the nearby shore. At the far side of this, across an arched stone bridge, Aldrick could see an inn. It was a welcome sight.

Télia drew her mare to a halt and turned to face him. "We will rest there tonight. For us a manmade shelter will prove safer than the trees."

He came to her side.

"What about the owners?" he asked. "If we are being hunted isn't it best we stay away from people — keep them safe?"

"We will warn them. We will say only that there may be danger about, not that you are hunted. If there is any trouble, they will have a cellar to take refuge in, and I will be ready."

"Do we even have weapons strong enough to defeat a ka-zchen if one does attack?"

"I have an aera's crossbow," Télia said with a thoughtful frown. "With an accurate shot it should be powerful enough to kill one. I cannot say for certain, though." She looked across at him. "You are the only one here who has survived an attack. Perhaps you should protect me."

"I can teach you how to run really fast if you like."

She laughed. Somehow she looked even more beautiful when she laughed. Her whole face was a smile. His heart melted.

When they arrived outside the inn the daylight was beginning to fade. The inn was small and looked very old, ancient even. Similar to Aldrick's home, its walls were built of stone, but over the years these had been weathered and, in places, had collapsed. One entire corner was reinforced with sturdy lengths of wood from the surrounding forest. Above the door, a faded sign hung from rusted chains reading 'Seawood Inn'.

They dismounted and led their horses round to a smelly, drab stable. There was little feed and the lack of other horses occupying the stalls made them question whether the inn had been abandoned. This soon proved not to be the case as, upon entering, an aged man with a walking stick greeted them from behind a dusty counter.

"Hello, weary travellers," he said brightly. "My name is Roan. Welcome to my humble inn." He gestured around with a shaky hand. "Are you looking to stay the night? I can offer you suitable bedding for little coin."

"Yes, please. We will have a room each, thank you," said Télia.

Roan looked surprised. "Oh, you are not a couple?" He scratched his chin. "Well now, I only have one room. It's quite spacious, mind you. Er, perhaps you can convince this young man to make do with the floor." He stared at Aldrick expectantly.

"One room will be fine," said Télia, reaching for her coin pouch. "We are just grateful to have a roof over our heads tonight. There has been talk of foul beasts prowling this area. We caught wind of this in Rain and have stopped here tonight as a precaution."

"Really... beasts you say?" Roan didn't sound alarmed by this at all. "Well, I'm sure you will find no such things shall pester you here. Never in all my years has there been an incident. Unless you bring the trouble with you, I believe we shall all have a very incident-less night."

Aldrick felt guilty. He knew that if there was a kazchen out there it would not pause at the walls of the inn to find him.

"Still, it would be wise to remain cautious," he said, glancing at Télia. "You never know what might be lurking out there in the shadows."

Roan eyed them both curiously.

"For such fine young souls you are very chary indeed," he remarked. "Nevertheless, I shall heed your words and I too will be wary of the shadows."

After Télia had paid him a small fee, the innkeeper showed them to the room. It was spacious but rather bare. An old bed stood against the left wall. A deer skin rug lay at its foot and a small wooden table stood beside it. There was no chair. To the right were a row of empty shelves and a tall wardrobe that slanted because of one broken leg. A single window directly opposite the door offered fresh air. They lay their possessions on the floor by the bed, not bothering to unpack. They would leave for Farguard at dawn.

Télia threw Aldrick an apple before drawing a small crossbow from her saddlebag. It looked to be a fine weapon. Its stock and foregrip were fashioned from a dark wood, the tree from which he could not say. The remainder was metal—steel or silver. Bands of intricate engravings decorated its barrel and limb. For such a deadly weapon it looked rather elegant. She set it beside the bed, removed her cloak and lay down. Aldrick remained standing, pondering. The journey had begun abruptly and there were still many questions he wished to ask this woman that he had not yet found the right moment for. Maybe this was it.

"Télia, who hired you to protect me?" he asked. She didn't respond so he went on. "Do they know why Selayna wants me dead?"

Télia sat back up and looked at him. She seemed settled now, more so than him at least.

"I assume they must know," she said pensively. "They definitely thought it was important to send me. Usually they would have assigned a job like this to someone far more experienced, but it was clearly urgent and I was already travelling south. They said they were sending other aeras, too. I have rarely heard of someone being appointed more than one. They must have known that the threat to you was great."

"Aera? That is what you are called?"

"Yes, it means 'guardian' in old Narthtongue."

"Why were you travelling south?"

"Actually, I was on my way to Jon's. I was told that watching over him would be an easy assignment, to finish my training. I doubt they expected he would ever be in any real danger. As far as I am aware he is not commonly known of these days."

"You were to protect him because he is a wielder?"

"Yes."

"But why would anyone want to protect me?" Aldrick asked, mystified. "I am no wielder. I am not… special or important."

A mysterious smile grew on Télia's face.

"You really don't know who you are, do you?" she asked, eying him.

"Something is telling me I don't…"

She surveyed him for a moment longer, then rested back against the headboard of the bed. "You know, when I was ordered to protect you, the name I was given was Aedimon. You are not known by that name in Rain?"

"Aedimon," Aldrick repeated curiously. "No, though I was adopted as a baby."

"I see."

"Wait, if you were given the wrong name, how did you know I was the one you were looking for?"

Télia's eyes twinkled.

"I have my ways," she said slyly then, changing the subject, "So how is it that you know Jon? I find that oddly coincidental."

"I knew him growing up. He is an old friend of my par… foster parents. My foster father, Braem, left to see him after the ka-zchen attacked me. I think they both know something about me, about my real parents. Maybe they were the Aedimons."

"I think you may be correct," said Télia. "I believe Jon will have the answers you seek."

"He truly is a wielder?"

She nodded. "Yes."

Aldrick pondered. Why had his life been shrouded

in secrecy? He began to wonder about his birth parents. Who had they been? Maybe they weren't simple merchants or farmhands as he had always imagined. He would know soon enough.

Gentle rain began to fall. The evening had faded to darkness. Roan kindly gave them a number of candles which they set on the table to provide some lighting. Although the threat of an attack lingered, the mood lightened and their conversation soon turned to stories of their upbringings. Aldrick recounted childhood memories of living against the mountains, of exploring the forests, of hunting and farming. Télia kept her stories rather brief, always more eager to hear his own. She told of a childhood raised in Daraki' Anya, a village neighbouring a larger city, Galdrem. He knew of Galdrem, of course. It was the capital city of the Narathlands, located in Morn, one of the northernmost provinces. She had been born the daughter of a high council member and had chosen her line of work because it offered travel, adventure, an escape from the monotony of day-to-day life. He reasoned they were similar in this respect—their dreams were not bound by the horizon.

While she spoke, Aldrick gazed upon Télia. Her beauty shone in the candlelight. She had removed her tunic and sat with blankets wrapped around her. He lay on his side across the end of the bed. Gradually gravity seemed to change direction, compelling him toward her, but he resisted. Though intoxicatingly alluring, her presence was unnerving, her beauty and grace daunting. Besides, there were currently far more concerning events unfolding. She had other things on her mind, some of which she had not voiced.

In time the soft patter of the rain made Aldrick drowsy. Télia kindly allowed him space beside her to lie down and stretch his legs. She remained sitting, seemingly restless once more. Her breaths were heavy and without rhythm.

"You should get some sleep," he said, eying her.

She yawned and shook her head. "No, I'm all right. Don't worry about me."

He did worry. Télia struck him as someone who was too good, who would push herself too far. It was her call though.

"Suit yourself," he said and closed his eyes.

Télia sprang from the bed.

He bolted upright. "What is it?!"

She put a finger to her lips. An anxious pause followed.

"I heard hooves on the road," she whispered.

He leapt to his feet and drew a knife from his belt.

"Keep quiet," she urged, loading her crossbow carefully. "This is trouble."

They made their way slowly toward the entrance of the Inn, keeping their figures stooped. Roan had gone to bed, but a number of lanterns still burned. Beyond the windows it was pitch black. Aldrick listened for any noise but could hear only the rain. They crept behind the counter and rested their backs against it. He looked to Télia. Her face was one of ardent concentration.

They waited.

"Maybe it was nothing," he said after a while.

Télia shook her head. "No, those who come in silence are not of good will."

There was a creak as the front door began to open slowly. Roan must have forgotten to lock it! Télia touched his shoulder and mouthed the words "Don't move."

He didn't.

"Be silent, he could still be awake," one intruder muttered to another.

Télia took the hand Aldrick held his knife in, turned it so that the blade was upright and gave him a subtle nod. He knew what she meant by it—he was going to need to use it.

Without warning Télia stood and aimed her crossbow beyond the counter.

"Move one step closer and die!" she yelled, then ducked all of a sudden. A knife flew into the wall behind her. She released an arrow then dropped back down beside him. Aldrick heard one of the intruders charging. As they reached the side of the bar he sprang up and drove the knife at their chest. It pierced armour but not flesh. Aldrick was gripped and thrust into the wall. Dazed, he lost his footing and collapsed to the floor, dropping his knife. Staring up, he saw a figure— a man shrouded in black—raising a sword. Télia came at him from behind but he whirled round and hit her hard across the face. She flew sideways to the floor.

"Télia, get up!"

She groaned. The man approached her, sniggering. Aldrick had to do something fast. His knife lay near him, and he took hold of it. As the man raised his sword, intent upon driving Télia's body through, Aldrick leapt at him, thrusting it into his side where the armour failed to protect. They both toppled to the floor. Aldrick sprang back up. The man remained down. He was dead, his sword still clutched in hand.

Once more the rain was the only sound to be heard. Aldrick stood shaking. By the entrance a second man lay with one of Télia's arrows in his chest, dead also.

Télia found her feet at Aldrick's side.

"Thanks," she said, rubbing her jaw.

"Yeah," he managed. He had just killed somebody. They were dead.

"You had to do it, Aldrick," Télia said, surveying him. "He would have killed us both." She went to the door and peered outside for a moment, checking for any further danger, then beckoned Aldrick back to the bedroom. In the hallway Roan stood with a lantern in his hand, staring at them with wide eyes.

"Fret not, my friend," Télia said to him as they passed. "They were enemies. The coast is clear now. We will deal with this in the morning. We apologise for causing you distress."

Roan said nothing, just watched them pass then looked vacantly down at the bodies lying upon the floor.

Aldrick slumped onto the bed. He was in no mood for anything. Télia sat down next to him.

"We should think no more of this night until

52

morning," she said quietly. "Let us rest now." She blew out the last burning candle.

They shared the bed. Télia slept but Aldrick could not. He lay on his back, dazed and subdued in the dark. The night was long.

5

STORM

Coldness had seeped into Aldrick's bones by morning. His body was exhausted, overtired. His mind was no better. They had risen early for there was unavoidable work to be done before they departed—the bodies of the intruders had to be removed. Télia asked him to help examine them first.

Easily visible, engraved into the men's cuirasses, was the outline of the same butterfly that had been branded on the ka-zchen which attacked him. He noticed now that their wings were outlandishly jagged and appeared profoundly sinister. The cuirasses enhanced this look as they too had a sharp, menacing look about them. From their plated pauldrons the men wore capes which also bore Selayna's sign.

There was nothing of great interest in their possession, only some gold which he and Télia chose to leave, and their swords. These were uniquely fashioned with long, thin blades and no cross-guards.

Télia said they would attract unwanted attention so they left them too. The men's horses had bolted in the night.

"They were aera servants of Selayna," said Télia, getting back to her feet. "Only they would wear her sign."

Aldrick found himself more concerned with how these men had tracked them to the inn.

"If they have been hunting me they might have found my family first!" he exclaimed. "We have to go back and see that they are safe!"

"No. These aeras would have been well behind the pace of the ka-zchen. They probably only arrived in the south yesterday, seeking to confirm it had already killed you. Even if they had been to Rain they would have avoided unnecessary altercation."

Aldrick remained apprehensive but trusted in Télia's judgement. He still felt she was keeping things from him but was willing to let this go, presuming they were things that mustn't need urgent utterance.

They buried the aeras behind the stables and did what they could to conceal the tracks leading to their shallow graves.

"If this had happened in the heart of the wilderness I would probably have left them where they fell," said Télia, raising one last patch of trodden grass with her foot. "Here, we must leave no evidence of our passing."

Back inside the inn they washed all blood from the floor, then Télia gave Roan generous gold and apologised profusely for what had occurred. The innkeeper was shaken but understanding and agreed not to notify any officials of the incident.

They departed immediately after eating and continued on their way along the woodland road toward Farguard. The rain had ceased in the early hours of the morning and the air was fresh and cool. Their pace was a trot. Télia didn't think there would be any more imminent danger.

"How are you feeling?" Aldrick heard her ask him after about an hour of travel.

He lifted his eyes from the road.

"I'm all right. I… it just didn't feel right," he murmured. His mind had been swamped in murky, black water—an endless flood of images of that aera lying on the floor with his knife lodged in him, lifeless.

Télia looked on with a faraway expression.

"Killing never feels right," she said sombrely. "Try not to dwell on it, Aldrick. It was them or us."

He tried not to but couldn't help it.

"Had you killed before?" he asked.

She shifted uncomfortably in her saddle. "Let us talk no more of this. The day is new, the air is fresh. We may as well enjoy the journey."

Aldrick looked at her and wondered what stories about herself she had kept unknown to him. He wondered how such a fair and kind young woman had come to wield the ability to take life. Perhaps one day she would tell him. He hoped they would still know each other in times beyond whatever lay ahead of them now.

They came into view of Farguard in the early afternoon. The woodland trees had given way to patchwork fields of yellow and brown. Beyond them, a wooden wall which bounded the village loomed. Overshadowing all else though were the mighty Midland Ranges. The procession of twin peaks towered so tall that their tips were obscured in cloud. A narrow valley lay between them that Aldrick assumed made passage to Jon's home. From it, a small river ran which passed through Farguard and on to the ocean. In the distance, the shoreline veered westward and eventually faded from sight behind a haze of salty sea air.

A lowered wooden gate offered them entrance into the village. Though there were no guards stationed outside, it somehow felt less welcoming than Rain. A dreary atmosphere hung over the place like heavy mist. The streets were boggy and the state of the housing was less than grand. Years had passed since they had last received caring attention. Many had been abandoned entirely. Wooden boards were nailed across their doors and windows and ivy engulfed their walls. The few dwellers who wandered the streets dressed mainly in long, cotton garments that were muddied at the bottom. There was little colour to be seen anywhere.

Aldrick and Télia led their horses to some rickety stables, paid to have them well fed and groomed, then made their way to the markets to buy food. They found little variety of choice. After reluctantly purchasing stale bread and some soft fruit from an unseemly woman with oily grey hair, Télia suggested they pay a visit to the local blacksmith.

"With the enemies we encountered last night we are going to need our own swords," she said.

Besides wooden ones, Aldrick had barely even held a sword in his life. It hadn't been necessary. He was a little hesitant. Télia said she would pay for his. He assumed her work paid generously as her coin pouch was still robust, even after bribing Roan the innkeeper that morning.

There was just one smith in the village: 'The Drunken Anvil'. It offered only a small selection of swords, so Télia bought them each a plain steel longsword with a leather-bound hilt. Hers was a woman's size—a little shorter and thinner than his own, which, with the tip against the ground, reached to his waist and was unnecessarily heavy. Each sword came with a leather sheath and strap which they fastened to their belts. It tired Aldrick just walking with his at his side. This amused Télia, who appeared very able with her own.

They thanked Torran the smithy before making their way to a small garden area by the riverside to eat lunch. The garden was overcome by a thicket of tangled weeds and the tree at the centre stood grey and leafless. Regardless, it was a fitting place for them to rest and discuss their imminent actions.

"We must be hasty," said Télia, biting into a pear. "I want to reach Jon's before nightfall."

Aldrick also anticipated arriving at Jon's. He hoped

they might also meet Braem there and learn from both of them the true reasons why he had been swept away on this whirlwind journey.

While they ate, he noticed Télia had begun to act strangely. She kept peering around and then pausing, as if she was listening for something. He listened too. He heard nothing out of the ordinary, just the gentle chant of the river and a cow mooing in a field somewhere beyond the village walls.

Suddenly she grabbed his arm and pointed toward two figures, each accompanied by a horse, walking down the main street from the far end of the village. "Look, Aldrick! It's a wielder. Maybe it's Jon!"

It was indeed Jon… and Braem! Relief swept over Aldrick. They were a welcome sight.

"Yes, it's Jon and my father!" he exclaimed, jumping to his feet.

They made their way to them. Braem noticed Aldrick as they approached and met him half way with an expression of surprise and bewilderment upon his weary face.

Aldrick embraced him. "Hello, Father."

"Aldrick… it is good yet surprising to see you here."

Jon came striding toward them, his wild, silvery mane a vivid contrast to the otherwise bleak surroundings.

"Ah, Aldrick, the man of the hour," he said brightly. "We were just on our way to visit you, my boy." He looked to Télia. "And you, aera, I have been expecting you for some time now. It appears, though, that you have found… one more in need than I." He winked at her. She didn't reply but offered him a subtle smile. Jon now returned his attention to Aldrick, resting a hand on his shoulder. "My boy, it seems you are caught up in a right mess, oh yes. I've heard all about the ka-zchen attack. It is very bothersome and I do fear it means more bother." He turned to Braem. "Now that we find ourselves together we must discuss matters—have young Aldrick here enlightened to the situation. As he and the aera were undoubtedly on their way to my home, we may as well return there."

Although he was lively, Aldrick sensed that Jon was unsettled, on edge, harried by thoughts.

Braem didn't respond to Jon. He was looking upon Aldrick with caring eyes. In them, Aldrick saw the same repressed fear that was there the night of the ka-zchen attack.

"I trust you have not been followed," Jon asked Télia after failing to receive a reply from Braem.

She shook her head. "No, we haven't. We had some trouble at an inn on the way here but that trouble is gone now."

"Brilliant!" Jon cried. "Now, we must be on our way. There are important things to discuss, shocking revelations to be revealed… I'm assuming you haven't spoilt anything for him?" He shot a gleeful glance at Aldrick.

"As little as I can. I was saving that for you." Télia looked at Aldrick and pulled an awkward face. "There are some things I perhaps could have told you which I have not."

"I had my suspicions," Aldrick replied. "I won't hold any of it against you, Télia." He had grown tired of wondering now, tired of guessing the answers to the many questions he had. All he wanted was to reach Jon's and hear whatever there was to be heard.

"Jon, I won't return with you," said Braem. "You have much to discuss with Aldrick. There is little more I can contribute."

Jon nodded. "Very good, my friend. Aldrick will be fine with me, and he has this lovely young aera watching over him now." He gestured to Télia.

"Good." Braem surveyed Aldrick. "Jon is to tell you very important things, some of which have been kept from you for far too long. Go with him now and be safe. Return to the farm when you are ready."

Aldrick nodded passively.

They embraced once more, then Braem eyed Télia. "You are protecting him? I trust in you to do so to the best of your ability."

"I will, sir," she said.

Braem gave Aldrick one final look, patted him on the shoulder then went on his way.

Aldrick felt only slight sadness watching him go. The point in his life had come where he could go on without relying on the comfort and closeness of his family. A new journey lay ahead of him.

In short time he and Télia, with Jon leading, had left the drowse of Farguard for the shelter of Jon's valley home. They rode swiftly, with purpose, along a wild path that followed the riverside deep into the heart of the cloud-cloaked ranges. As they passed more and more stream inlets the river gradually became a stream itself. Eventually it veered from the path to its origin in the mountaintops. Not far beyond this point the trees cleared and they emerged into a surprisingly vast opening claimed by small scrub bushes and tussocks. Here, the path forked. Jon led them left to where his house was situated against the edge of the clearing, behind a small incline that, with the help of a few stranded old trees, kept it from the view of passers-by.

It was a curious and magnificent dwelling, standing some feet above the ground upon an elevated wooden foundation. A polished landing traced its many walls. Unlike village housing, it had clearly not been constructed following the guidelines of tradesmen. The walls bulged in the centre where vertical planks of wood met each other. Windows were located in various places, high and low, and did not always have four sides. Most were covered by drapes on the inside. The roof had been lined with thin tree trunks that protruded well beyond the walls and was thatched with masses of straw. Aldrick had never seen a home quite like it.

Jon led them to a small stable to the right of the house where they dismounted their horses and offloaded their gear. Gusts of rain had begun sweeping down the valley, so he promptly showed them indoors whereupon he ran around lighting various lanterns and candles to counter the dwindling daylight. The interior of the house was roomy, made more so by the outward curving of the walls. Immediately left of the doorway was a kitchen area, bordered by a bench that was cluttered by parchment and various indiscernible belongings. Ahead of them was the living room. A large woollen rug covered much of its floor space. On the left was a comfortable-looking seating area with pillows and blankets and in the corner, an open fire. Along the walls, dark red and green drapes hung that were covered in strange patterns and symbols. Above them, accessible by a small stairway, was Jon's bedroom and study.

"This is home," Jon said, proudly walking back down the stairs after igniting one final lantern that hung from the centre of the ceiling.

"I love it!" exclaimed Télia, looking around in fascination and delight. "It's so different, and cosy."

Jon chuckled. "I'm glad you like it. Do not hesitate to make yourself at home, in whatever way that means for you. I imagine you will be staying a short while."

Aldrick wondered how long he meant.

Jon looked upon him with caring eyes. "Oh, Aldrick, you look so much like..." he paused momentarily, "like I remember you." He clapped his hands together. "Well now, let us relax, refresh ourselves and afterwards I shall see to supper. When our stomachs are full we will discuss much. Yes, indeed we shall!" He spoke with lofty spirits. This was how Aldrick remembered him—always acting in a manner that offset any seriousness there was. Never had he seen Jon's face grim. Since their last meeting, he had aged well. No more wrinkles had appeared on his face nor silver hairs upon his head; perhaps because they had always been silver. How very strange it was to be looking upon someone he had known all his life and only now knew was a wielder. Aldrick still saw no obvious clues that Jon was. Save for his mane of hair, he appeared nothing like the images Aldrick had in his mind of how one might—clad in grand robes, brandishing a magical wand. Jon was still the same quirky old man from the mountains.

After a short rest and cup of tea that was accompanied by idle talk, Jon left to fetch meat and potatoes to roast for dinner. Aldrick and Télia were left sitting in the living room. The fire had been lit and was a hypnotic dance of yellow flames upon the hearth. Although the mood was restful, Aldrick readily anticipated the conversation that approached. He would at last know why he was hunted. Why, after so long living a simple life, he was suddenly fleeing from death, having to take life to preserve his own. He had an uncanny feeling that this fate had always been pursuing him and he yearned to know where it would lead him from here.

Dinner came late but was plentiful. Jon had cooked more than enough for them all. The mutton and potatoes were roasted to perfection and accompanied by boiled vegetables and thick, nourishing gravy. They ate in silence, subdued by both keen appetites and a squall of thoughts. Outside, the mountainous world was at rest, lulled by the soft sound of the falling clouds.

When they had finished eating, Aldrick took it upon himself to break the silence.

"Sooo, here we are..." he started.

Jon sat back in his seat and made himself comfortable. "Yes, here we are. You have come a long way and I think it is about time you had some burning questions answered."

Aldrick waited breathlessly for him to continue.

Jon stroked his beard thoughtfully for some time. His natural soft smile had faded from his face. "As you are no doubt already aware, Aldrick, a certain wielder named Selayna has decided that she doesn't want you around. You have already encountered more than one of her servants. They travelled far to find you. You wonder why, yes? Well, first you must know some things about your birth parents... I knew them both well. Their names were Isobel and Gilthred." Jon looked away. His eyes glinted. "Aldrick, the things I am about to tell you are no ordinary things. I'm sure you won't find them easily acceptable as truth. However, they are. I have little reason to keep anything from you now." He took a deep breath. "Your parents were wielders. They were great wielders, some of the very greatest, in fact."

Aldrick's mind ground to a halt. "They... what?"

Jon lent forward. "Their son was a wielder too. Aldrick, *you* are a wielder."

What again? No, that wasn't right. He wasn't a wielder! "No, I'm not a wielder, Jon. You must be confused. I'm just... ordinary... I am!" He looked at Télia for some kind of reassurance, but it appeared that this had not been news to her.

"I'm quite sure you are, my dear boy!" cried Jon. "As sure as the mountains rise you are. And that's just the beginning of it!"

His mouth hung half open. "H... how am I a wielder?"

"How? Well, because your parents were, obviously! Wielders do not bear humans. You are as much a human as you are a rabbit."

"How is it that I know nothing of this, then?!"

"Because you have not been told. Well, at least not until now."

This conversation was impossible. Aldrick was only just becoming accustomed to living in a world where wielders existed. Being one himself was a whole different story. Surely he had been grievously misinformed. He shook his head fervently. He was on his feet, tense. "It's not true!"

"Aldrick, be calm," Télia said gently. "I knew this myself, but it was news that needed to come to you from one more understanding and knowledgeable than myself. Jon is very wise. Heed his words."

Jon chuckled. "Wise? I don't consider myself as such. I'm just old, far too old... now where was I?" He pondered. "Ah yes, I know where I was. You are a wielder, my boy, as were your parents! Now your parents, Aldrick, they were very special. When I said that they were some of the greatest wielders, I referred not only to their noble characters but also to their stormpowers. Storm, of course, is the term given to the magic we possess. We are wielders of the storm. Many folk may simply refer to us as wizards or sorcerers, but wielder is the preferred title.

"Your parents were able to wield their stormpowers

in unique and exceptional ways. Your father, Gilthred, could influence the weather—turn the rain to sun and the wind into a weapon." Jon paused again, seemingly adrift in an ocean of memories. "And your mother, she could do something quite extraordinary. She could drain another wielder's storm from them. It was an ability feared by many." He looked upon Aldrick with grave eyes. "Aldrick, you are hunted because you are feared too, because you also have this ability."

Aldrick fell back to a seated position. Jon's words continued to numb his mind. How was any of this true? How had it been kept from him for so long? Since being swept away on this journey he had not even entertained the possibility of such truths being revealed. He had expected more trivial explanations for the attempts on his life. Perhaps they came as revenge for unpaid debts his parents owed to Selayna or something of the like. Never could he have foreseen that it was he who was considered a threat.

Télia came to him with a mug of water from the kitchen and placed it in his hands.

"The look on your face tells me many of your thoughts," she said, studying him. "Thoughts I am sure will take time to rationalise."

"Rationalise? None of this has a place in the realm of the rational!" he exclaimed. "Wizards, or wielders, as they are called—I was so used to imagining them in stories of old and distant lands. I never imagined they were a part of my own life. Jon, my parents… me? I am one of them?" He stared blankly forward, shaking his head at every impossible notion.

Télia sat beside him and rested a hand on his shoulder. "Just remember that nothing Jon or I tell you changes who you are. I know that sounds foolish but it's true. The whole ground doesn't disappear beneath your feet. You are the same person you have always been. Only, there is more to your story. Everyone you know, including me now, is ever willing to find your head upon their shoulders. I am your aera, Aldrick. I remain here—at your side."

Her words were kind and calming, though not nearly calming enough. Aldrick managed a faint smile of appreciation before his mind caved in to the weight of his thoughts once more.

"I will continue, if that is all right," said Jon, who had been observing him mindfully. "I understand that what I have said is difficult to accept, Aldrick, I do, but there is much more that needs telling, and there is no better time than now, with food in our bellies and the rain falling outside, to tell it."

Aldrick took a deep breath. "I'm listening."

"Excellent! But wait… I have lost myself yet again." Jon squinted down at the floor, stroking his beard. "Ah yes! You have the abilities your parents did! That is why Selayna wants you dead." His eyes widened. "Oh, but no. Selayna is not the one who wants you dead. Oh no. No, no, no! She does the bidding of another." He looked upon them gravely. "There is another who wishes your demise, one whom your parents knew well—Selayna's brother. His name is Malath."

Aldrick heard Télia gasp beside him. Cold radiated from her. There ensued a deathly silence in which only the faint flicker of flames and occasional crack of heated wood could be heard from the hearth.

"Malath is also a wielder?" Aldrick asked finally. "My parents knew him?"

"They did, only too well." Jon waved his hand aggressively and the fire roared, brightening the room and vanquishing the chill in the air. Aldrick stared. "He was their friend—a valued member of the wielding community. Malath Jayther, the great and damned foolish!" Jon's pacing quickened. Anger fuelled his steps. "Your parents trusted him with their lives, as anyone might have. No one had ever heard of such a distinguished wielder turning so foul. Arrogant—yes, but sour, bitter and resentful? No. No, Malath was one of a kind, a well-privileged idiot!" Jon halted and turned to Aldrick. "He led your parents to their doom."

Aldrick swallowed. He had often wondered about his parents of late, but only now did he realise that hearing their story inevitably meant learning how they died.

"Tell me what happened," he said.

Jon seated himself in an armchair by the fire.

"This all began many years ago," he started. "Gilthred, Isobel and Malath were scholars of Delthendra—the wielder's lyceum in Galdrem, a place Télia is familiar with I'm sure." Télia nodded. "Well, that is where they came to know each other. They were each very wise and astute, but Malath was more powerful, as was he ambitious. As a young man the Synod adopted him and—"

"Wait... the Synod?"

"The Synod is an order of 'highly esteemed' wielders in Galdrem. I was once associated with them myself."

Aldrick could tell Jon held no high opinion of them. "I see."

"As I was saying, they adopted Malath and installed him as chancellor of Delthendra. This gave him great power and position over not only novice wielders, but humans alike." Jon leaned forward. "You see, Aldrick, wielders once stood above humans. It is a common belief that our storm comprises half of our very being, but back then many claimed it to be the superior half.

"So, Malath being promoted to chancellor meant that he suddenly had command over a vast majority of the peoples in the land. He even held sway over the high council. They were advised to follow his guidance on all matters of social and political discourse. The system was egregiously flawed. All the time though, it was the elder wielders of the Synod who pulled Malath's strings.

"In following years they became more accepting of humans' rightful place as equals among them. They sought a democratic society, a peaceful one. But as much as their arrogance lessened, Malath's grew. He feared that these new ways of thinking would threaten his position as chancellor. Resentment grew in him, a dark fire that could not be doused. Madness took hold. Members of the Synod began to disappear inexplicably. Common folk were found dead in the streets, murdered by storm.

"Your parents soon realised that Malath was responsible for this, along with Selayna and his ever faithful, brainwashed scholars. Though it was hard for them to accept, he had become an unspeakable force of evil. Like themselves, he possessed a unique ability no other wielder did. He could defy death, manipulate it... reverse it. He threatened to use this to 'cleanse' the Narathlands of the filth of humanity.

"He planned to venture to Darkna—a hallowed temple of old which stands at the edge of the legendary Vuldenfar Chasm. There, a great power exists that would greatly strengthen his storm, allowing him to resurrect an entire army of ancient warriors from the Life Afterwards to carry out his murderous intent.

"Your parents knew they needed to act, but knew also that it would be futile to confront Malath on a level battleground. In his madness, his powers had been rendered ever stronger than before. Their options were few."

Jon raised a finger. "But, as fortune might have it, some months earlier Gilthred had stumbled across an invaluable object while on a scholarly expedition in the west—a peculiar stone, one with a profound attribute. It could hold storm within it. They discovered this when Isobel practised her sapping ability on Gilthred while holding the stone in hand. Typically, his storm would soon have returned to him, but this time it did not. It had been absorbed into the stone. For days they tried to retrieve it, but to no avail. The stone was of the hardest material known to them and could not be penetrated.

"For a time they attempted to conceal the fact that Gilthred's storm was lost to him, but inevitably this was exposed, though no one was able to offer a plausible explanation nor a solution. Not even the eldest and wisest of the Synod could unravel the stone's mystery.

"While it had caused them such inconvenience, its power gave your parents an idea—perhaps it could be used to entrap Malath's storm. This was the only way to permanently remove him as a threat to the Narathlands and punish him for his blind self-righteousness. They confronted him at Darkna. I was there—one of the wielders delegated to safeguard the temple at the time, and the power held within.

"Words would not sway Malath from his intentions so Isobel did indeed drain his storm into the stone. While doing so, Gilthred and I shielded her from his followers. We defeated many, Selayna included, but your father, being without power, was overwhelmed." Jon eyed Aldrick sorrowfully. "Your father died fighting for the people of the Narathlands, Aldrick. He gave everything."

The room was silent. Aldrick couldn't speak. The world had fallen away around him.

"Isobel had successfully taken Malath's storm," Jon continued. "This terrified his followers, so they fled, whisking him away with them. It was the last time anyone saw any of them. Without Malath's power or position they were no longer seen as a threat to Galdrem. The Synod was confident that they would not return.

"Even so, there lingered the risk of a revenge attack on Isobel. She needed security but refused to stay in Galdrem. The loss of Gilthred had broken her. Only recently had she found out she was pregnant with you, Aldrick. She left the city and travelled south, to here, where she built a home for herself." Jon looked around. Tears glistened in his eyes. "She loved it here, Aldrick. This is where you were born."

Aldrick found tears in his own eyes. He wiped them away.

Jon rested his back against the chair and closed his eyes for a time before going on.

"An appointed aera and I had followed your mother here to watch over her, but she did not allow us to stay so we moved to Farguard. In time, the aera returned to Galdrem. I remained, wary that she might one day need my protection...

Jon swallowed heavily. "It was in the winter. You were a newborn. I had come here with supplies for her. When I arrived the house was ablaze. She was inside. I doused the flames and pulled her from it but... I was too late. She was..." Jon took a moment.

"I thought all had been lost that day Aldrick, but it wasn't. With the raging noise now subsided, I heard your cry from within the trees. Your mother had hidden you there, tucked in a blanket. You were safe. I am uncertain if those who came for her were aware you existed. I knew then that you must be protected. It was my responsibility. The only way to be sure you were safe was to see that your identity remained a secret. You couldn't be known by your father's name, Aedimon, nor could you stay with me. I took you to Rain, a village with no prior connection to you or your parents. Braem and Phelvara adopted you there. I remained here and rebuilt your mother's house, to preserve her memory. But I could never quite let it go, Aldrick. That is why I would visit you as you grew up. Being such lovely people, Braem and Phelvara said that I was always welcome. Eventually I told them everything but made them swear never to tell you, only to come to me if I was ever needed... and here we are today."

Aldrick lifted his eyes from the floor. Everything was out of focus and glistening. He felt sick and heavy. Above all other thoughts and questions, imagery of Gilthred and Isobel—his parents—flooded his mind. Both murdered, his mother in this very home. Slowly an emotion he was unfamiliar with began to seep through him. So much had been stolen from him! He rose and left the room.

Solitude found him outside. He stood a short distance from the house among the tussocks, fists clenched and head raised to the skies. Rain quietly fell upon him. Around him the mountains cowered, hiding their heads in the clouds. He let out a cry of rage and lightning erupted around him. Simultaneously thunder roared, ricocheted off the mountains and made the ground tremble beneath his feet.

6

TRAINING

Aldrick closed the door quietly behind him. He felt much calmer now. Jon and Télia were standing together in silence. The loose ends of a smile lingered on Jon's face. Télia's was a tone lighter than usual. He walked past them and seated himself by the fire.

"Frightful weather outside, is it not?" Jon asked.

"It is."

"Your father's storm surges within you, Aldrick"

Aldrick looked up. "Hold on… are you saying… I did that? I made the thunder and lightning?"

"You surely did. None of those clouds out there are storm clouds. That was of your own making."

"But… but how? How is it that my father, my mother and Malath all had these abilities that other wielders don't?"

"An intuitive question," Jon said, raising a finger. "It is perhaps what brought them together at a young age—their uniqueness. It occurs in those who have survived great peril in their lives, who have persevered through immeasurable odds. In doing so they inherit the ability to control whatever it was that threatened their survival. As I recall, your father came to the Narathlands from a neighbouring realm. On his journey he was caught in a ferocious storm at sea, the likes of which few have ever witnessed. The vessel carrying him was destroyed but the tide carried him ashore. It was soon after he awoke that he discovered he possessed the heightened ability to manipulate the weather.

"Your mother, well, she never talked about it much, but when she was young, on an expedition into the western lands, she was captured by a wielder savage who held her captive and tortured her. This was until a group of aeras tracked her down and rescued her. From then on she was able to take another wielder's storm, so as never to be harmed again..."

"And Malath?"

"Malath." Jon scowled. "I understand he drowned when swimming as a child. Had he not been revived by a stranger he would have remained in the Life Afterwards. Unfortunately for us though, he gained the ability to sway death itself and went on to become the monster he is."

"So he has evaded his own death twice now. He was left standing at Darkna? Even after being rendered powerless?"

"Yes. He was your parents' friend, Aldrick. They never wanted to take his life. Besides, back then the act of one wielder killing another was a crime worse than murder. It was those very events—the treason of Malath, Selayna and their followers—that finally saw the abandonment of that law. Only then was it realised how truly far a noble wielder could descend into madness and that only wielders themselves could defend the people, should it happen again."

"And now, Malath has learnt of my existence and wants me dead… because I am the only one who can kill him, because I was born with my mother's ability."

"Well, yes, Aldrick. It is unclear to me how any other wielder might best him without such a rare advantage. His powers are too great."

"I don't understand how this has come to be, though. How does Malath have his storm again, after losing it to the stone?"

Jon heaved a sigh. "I cannot say. I became aware of this only when Braem told me of the brand on the ka-zchen that attacked you—Selayna's brand. Only Malath could have returned her from death and only she could have breathed new life into it. It is the sole explanation I am afraid." He rested an elbow on his knee and stroked his silvery beard broodingly. His demeanour was that of someone who was deeply troubled, who knew dark things were ahead.

"If Malath is all powerful again, that's perfect. I will see he is finished with, for good this time, and whoever chooses to follow him."

Jon's eyes lifted. "You would seek vengeance, Aldrick? I did not expect it of you. All these years you have been oblivious to so much yet now, when truths come to light, you act as if it all happened yesterday."

Suddenly fresh waves of anger and resentment swept through Aldrick. "You! Why did you never seek revenge for my parents' murders? Were you afraid? I thought wielders were supposed to be noble, courageous!"

Every morsel of Jon's face became a frown. "It would have changed nothing, Aldrick. I let it go because of you—so you could have a life free of all this, and so I could be there for you if you ever needed me. I hoped you never would. Clearly it was not meant to be so."

Aldrick looked down at his feet, realising he had crossed a line he shouldn't have.

There was an uncomfortable silence until finally Télia spoke.

"Tea, anyone?" she asked politely.

"Yes please," he and Jon replied as one.

He knew he ought to apologise. "Jon, I'm—"

"It's all right, my boy," Jon said heartily, casting negativity aside. His frown had disappeared. "You are taking all this much better than could be expected. Learning of your parents' fate and that you are a wielder, well... I can't quite imagine."

"Well, the wielder part isn't so bad."

Jon chuckled. "Just you wait, my boy."

It was late now. They arranged seating in an arc around the fire and sat in silence, staring into the nonchalant flames. Télia's brew of tea was the best Aldrick had tasted—strong and bitter, with the aroma of a spring meadow lingering somewhere in the background. As he drank he felt strange. Accepting all that Jon had told him now came with ease, though much of it remained foreign to him. He was in uncharted waters and did not know the ropes.

Télia sat close at Aldrick's side. She was without tea and appeared anxious. He imagined she feared for her family and homeland. He wanted her to somehow be at peace.

"It's all right," he said, nudging her softly. "Everything will be. I'm going to make sure of it."

She nodded and offered up an unconvincing smile.

Jon was eying Aldrick with a faint smile of his own. "You are indeed your parents' son. They would be very proud."

"Surely the Synod is aware of Malath's return," said Télia, now voicing her qualms. "That is why I was repurposed to protect Aldrick. I was sent word on my journey here to do so without hesitation."

Jon sipped his tea. "Oh, I am quite certain they are well aware. Malath was always one to flaunt his power. He has probably paraded himself through the streets of Galdrem."

"But he can't be left free to continue his old plans!" cried Télia. "I grew up in fear of him, even as a powerless outcast. What he intended to do—slay humanity—that's unthinkable! Would the Synod stand idle and see that happen?!"

"Let us hope not. They were wise enough to presume Aldrick would become a target."

"And what of the Shard of Heart's Storm? Is it adequately guarded?"

"After Malath's first attempt to gain access to it nearly succeeded—the attempt Aldrick's parents foiled—the holding chamber was sealed with the most powerful of warding enchantments, one not even he can break."

"The Shard of Heart's Storm. That is the great power in the temple you mentioned earlier?" Aldrick asked, feeling increasingly distanced from the span of his knowledge.

Jon nodded. "Yes, in the Temple Darkna. You see, it is a common belief among wielders that our storm originates from the heart of the world. Some wielders believe it religiously so. The Shard is a piece of that heart. It was found deep in a mine over a thousand years ago; the only piece ever unearthed."

"That's incredible... the thought that our world is founded on some great body of storm. If just a shard bears such power, imagine what power lies within the heart itself..."

"A thought many wielders have entertained. But come, now is not the time to linger on it. Télia's fear that Malath seeks to acquire the Shard and fulfil his evil desires is not without warrant. There is no doubt in my mind that he will try to find a way into its holding chamber. He is far too ambitious not to. If he cannot achieve it by his own hand he will find the necessary means to."

"So we must do something," said Télia urgently.

Jon looked flustered. "Yes, yes. But exactly what is the question."

"Well, it's clear I have my part to play," said

Aldrick. "I will use my mother's ability in the same way she did to trap Malath's storm."

"But the stone she used was the key. Without that, you could never withhold his storm long enough to allow a reliable chance to strike, and you would find yourself rendered defenceless in the attempt. Your mother had barely mastered wielding that ability herself. You have yet to learn even the most basic of wielding techniques."

"I made thunder and lightning," argued Aldrick.

"Yes, but that was with your emotions flowing freely. Occasions like that are incredibly rare."

"Oh," he said, feeling somewhat disenchanted. "So we need the stone then."

"Absolutely, I won't have you go blundering after Malath without it."

"What happened to it after Darkna?"

"The damned Synod claimed it, declared it a rare magical artefact and locked it in Delthendra's museum. That's what happened to it," fumed Jon "It was exhibited as 'The Halfstone — the stone that stole a wielder's stormhalf'. They failed to conceive what a threat it still posed. Not a year passed before it was stolen, most likely by one of Malath's faithful, perhaps Malath himself. That was the day any lasting faith I bestowed in the Synod was lost, and another reason I chose to remain here, away from their witlessness. Wise they may be, but insightful? Oh no."

"Wait, if Malath has probably had his hands on the stone all this time, why is it not until recently that he has found a way to retrieve his storm?"

Jon shrugged. "As I have said, I do not know how he's done it... and I'm not so sure I want to."

"We must find out," stressed Télia. "It may yet work as it did for Isobel."

"Yes. It seems to be the brightest hope we have at the moment." Jon looked at them both gravely. "You do realise that if we were to find the stone, this all boils down to a confrontation with Malath?"

Aldrick gritted his teeth. "That's what I'm hoping for. Do you know where he is, Jon? Surely twenty years has not passed without word of his whereabouts."

"Well, no one has seen him. But it is believed he fled to the Blackbed Plains, to the north of here."

"Blackbed... I have heard that name before, in stories."

"Many have. It is a sinister land, one of the last few places in the Narathlands where evil yet thrives. Only those with nasty, dark hearts find refuge there. It would be of no surprise to me if that is where Malath and Selayna dwell. Before she died, Selayna occupied an ancient fort there where she claimed to be researching the mysteries of the area for 'academic purposes'." Jon clenched his fists and the fire began to roar once more.

"We would need an army to infiltrate a place like that!" exclaimed Télia. "I have heard stories of aeras venturing there and never returning home."

"I'm afraid we are on our own," Jon said glumly. "I could request the Synod unites what remains of the wielders in Galdrem, but I doubt they would support such a venture unless it was proven that Malath poses a direct and imminent threat."

"Well it's worth a try, isn't it?" Télia stood up. Her face was lit by the blaze of the fire. Her hair wavered in the heat. "All my life I have trained to protect wielders under the Synod's command. I refuse to believe that they would do so little in the face of adversity. You must warn them of what is coming, Jon!"

"I will try, but expect my words to fall on deaf ears."

Télia sat down again, huffing. Jon looked on into the fire. There was a lengthy silence. Aldrick felt tiredness lulling his eyes closed. Télia had crescents under her own. She had slept even less than him over the past few days.

"Perhaps it is time for us all to rest," he suggested.

"True wisdom right there," Jon said, rising and stretching. "We will speak more of all this tomorrow. If you are feeling up to it, Aldrick, I will teach you how to wield your storm in the morning, at least, get some of the basics out of the way."

Aldrick nodded. "Please."

Jon showed Télia to a spare bed through a doorway to the right of the living room. Aldrick remained put. In accompaniment with the woollen rug, there were enough blankets and cushions for him to find comfort upon the floor by the fireside. When Jon returned he waved his hand and the flames dwindled to a smoulder.

"Goodnight, my boy," he said before retiring upstairs, extinguishing lamps and candles as he went.

"Goodnight." Aldrick rolled onto his side and closed his eyes. He was too tired to think anymore.

The morning arrived sooner than Aldrick hoped, though not before a surreal dream in which he told a little black fantail that he was leaving on an adventure. The adventure consisted of repeatedly falling from the cliff behind the family home, though this time he was unaware of the cause. Each time he landed at the bottom unscathed, where Kaal met him with a grin and words of encouragement. When he woke from this dream, it took a moment for the words he, Jon and Télia had shared last night to come flooding back into his mind. He lay on his back, assuring himself that he had truly woken, then heaved himself to his feet. This was all real. Here he stood—in the wielder Jon's living room, far from the place he called home and the family he held dear. Here he stood—a wielder himself.

Aldrick was not the first to have risen. The front door was ajar. A cool breeze met him, bringing with it the cleansing smell of damp earth after rainfall. He wandered to the kitchen where he found a small loaf of bread that he claimed for breakfast, then made his way outside. Much of yesterday's clouds had dispersed and the golden peaks of the surrounding mountains were visible. Trees stopped growing less than one hundred paces above where he stood. The path they had followed to reach Jon's had been on a gradual incline all the way from Farguard. He was now at a higher elevation than the family home was against the

Mountains Rain. Isobel had truly chosen an isolated place to live. It was here she had intended to raise him...

"Good morning Aldrick." Télia was walking toward him from within the nearby trees. She looked lovely, as always. Beams of morning sunlight shone through the canopy and danced gracefully upon her, accentuating her natural beauty.

Butterflies tickled his insides.

"Hello. You're up..." He realised he hadn't formed a complete sentence. "Early," he quickly added.

She smiled. "It comes with the job. I've been on guard since before the dawn. Wielders tend to die in the dark, when people can sneak up on them."

"That's comforting," he said sarcastically. "Thank you though—for being here."

"You're welcome."

For a moment they stood in silence.

"Sooo, no sign of anyone or anything evil out there?" he asked.

"None." Télia sat on a boulder next to him and stretched her neck.

Something that had stirred Aldrick's curiosity recently came back into his mind.

"Télia," he began. "How did you find me in the market place that day in Rain, before you learned my name? And in Farguard, you saw Jon and knew he was a wielder, even before meeting him."

She grinned up at him. "Ah, well, something which I may have failed to mention during our journey here is that aeras, as well as a rare few wild creatures, like ka-zchen, have the gift of sensing storm within a wielder. It is of great advantage to us as we remain aware of our wielder's whereabouts when they are out of eyesight."

"What does it feel like?" Aldrick asked, fascinated. "What do you feel as I stand here now?"

Télia looked at him contemplatively. "It is as though you radiate heat... but it is cool." She shook her head. "It's difficult to explain."

"Does it not get annoying—being around a wielder when you can always feel them?"

She shrugged. "We learn to live with it. It's like any sense I suppose. We can always see and we don't get sick of that, do we?"

"True... is the feeling more intense when we wield our storm?"

"Your storm will surge within you, but we cannot feel storm which has been spent, only when it is in its pure state."

"I see. Only people who have this gift are allowed to be aeras?"

"Yes..."

"Because an aera's job is solely to protect wielders. You are no ordinary bodyguard."

"No." Télia stood up. "Aldrick, I avoided mention of this on our journey here because it would have spoilt the big surprise for you. I saved that for Jon. I meant not to hide things from you. I shouldn't have... I'm sorry."

He smiled. "It's fine. Really."

"How are you coping with the whole 'being an

almighty wielder' thing, anyway?" she asked.

Considering this was daunting. He sighed and shrugged. "It's definitely new."

She laughed aloud. "Well you're very special, you know. Inheriting two unique abilities... many will be in awe of you."

Aldrick was sure, or at least convinced himself he saw Télia's eyes dart up and down his body. He hoped she was thinking what he hoped she was thinking.

"People might be in awe of me if I actually learn how to wield something," he said self-effacingly.

"Don't worry, Jon will train you well. And, if you also wish to learn how to wield your blade, I can teach you a thing or two. The better you are at defending yourself, the easier my job becomes."

"What if you're the one who needs defending?" he asked teasingly. "I recall it was so at Seawood Inn."

"True." Télia walking up to him and placed her hands firmly on her hips. "But only after I took down the first assassin and then took a fist to the face trying to save you."

"... True."

They stood staring into each other's eyes. Hers were like enchanted emeralds—alluring, spellbinding. His heart leapt beneath his chest, which was strange, for he was certain she had stolen it from him days earlier.

"Both early risers I see."

He turned. Jon had emerged from the house and was striding toward them, donning a grand robe. It was forest green with thin strings of deep blue symbols entangling it in intricate fern-like patterns. A fine band of gold lined the hood. This he wore down, keeping visible his wild mane of hair. He looked remarkably wielder-like.

Jon had noticed Aldrick staring.

"My robes?" he asked, peering down at them. "Yes, well, as we are going to be wielding today I thought I may as well look the part."

"You most certainly do!" exclaimed Télia. "It makes you look both noble and wise, Jon."

"Thank you, my dear," he replied humbly. "They have been well kept, though for far too long now. I am glad to be wearing them once again."

Télia took Jon by the arm. "Come, keep me company over breakfast."

His face lit up.

"What a charming idea," he said delightedly. "It would be my pleasure."

Télia turned back to Aldrick. "Will you join us?"

"No thanks. I'm enjoying the sun. You go and eat."

She shrugged. "Suit yourself."

They left, chatting, toward the house. Aldrick remained standing alone with his bread. Although heavy thoughts lingered in the recesses of his mind, he anticipated what this new day promised—opportunity to learn how to wield... at least, begin to learn. He tried to imagine how it was done, how it might feel. He couldn't recall feeling anything other than intense anger last night when the thunder and lightning occurred. He had done nothing physically, at least not knowingly, to induce it. Perhaps waving wands wasn't the way to do it in the real world.

While Aldrick pondered such things, he took time to explore the surrounding land. He wandered into the clearing, avoiding frequent patches of bog and thorn bushes. In the occasional hazard-free areas, tame mountain goat and sheep grazed. He supposed Jon was their herder and profited from their meat and milk. Further into the heart of the clearing, Aldrick stumbled across what appeared to be the remnants of a stone wall hiding within the grass. Curious, he followed it a short way to where he found a markedly large area where crumbled stones lay in ruin upon the ground, overgrown by mosses and leafless creeping vines. Some kind of fortress must have once stood here, many years ago. Intrigued by this, he decided he would ask Jon about it. When he returned he found Jon back outside by the stables.

"It was once a watchtower," Jon informed him, feeding the horses apples from a small sack. "Long ago, the Narathlands was a mighty, sprawling empire. This valley was the main way of passage between the capital city, Prithe, and the southern provinces. War saw the fall of the empire and the city in turn. This valley has long since been forgotten, as was the tower." Jon finished feeding the horses and turned to Aldrick. "You may be surprised at just how rich the history of the Narathlands is. It has not always been the peaceful place it appears today."

"It appears?"

"Evil lingers."

"So it does. I suppose that is why we are here."

"Yes. And why I must show you how to wield, my

boy." Jon turned and strolled toward the house.

Aldrick followed. "Shall we begin training soon?"

"Indeed. I suspect you are eager to learn?"

"Very," he replied excitedly. "I am ready when you are."

"Well then, just let me fetch a thing or two and we will be off. There is a secreted glade a little way into the forest where we can practice in the confidence that we shan't draw any unwanted attention. You never know who could be wandering the mountain path—servants of the enemy perhaps!"

Aldrick thought Jon sounded a little paranoid. "No one's going to find us all the way out here."

Jon wheeled around. "Words uttered by a fool! Do not make me retell you what happened to your mother in this very place!" He stormed inside.

Aldrick was left feeling immediate regret. The murder of his mother was a recent revelation to him. For Jon, it had been an unspeakable tragedy in his life. Jon had sought to protect her and held more resentment for her passing than could ever be understood.

Télia, who had been relaxing on the landing, stood and came to Aldrick.

"Don't take Jon's words too heavily," she said quietly. "The many years spent alone here have given him too much time to dwell on sad things."

"No, it was my own fault," Aldrick mumbled, annoyed with himself. "My words were thoughtless."

He made his way inside, where he found Jon removing a long, thin object wrapped in cloth from a wooden chest underneath the stairs.

"Jon, I—" he started, but was interrupted.

"There is no need to apologise, my boy," Jon said briskly. "It was I who spoke out of turn. Let us put it behind us and focus on the future." He pulled the cloth from the object. At first glance it appeared to be a walking stick, though there were notable differences. Instead of a conveniently carved grip at its head, there was a pale blue oval stone, about the size of crow's egg. This was fastened in place upon a gold collar. The shaft was fashioned from a dark wood. A strange spiralling pattern wound from end to end, interrupted midway by a leather-bound grip.

Aldrick gasped. "Is that—"

"Yes, this is a staff," said Jon, inspecting it closely. "Many years have passed since I last held it." He took the staff firmly in one hand and brandished it before him. Aldrick saw him now as not just a wielder, but a powerful one, one whose day was far from over. "Come, let us begin." Jon strode past Aldrick and out the door.

He and Télia followed Jon along a narrow, overgrown trail behind the house that led them a short way through the forest to a small glade. Here, the ground was unlike that at the centre of the valley. It was level and the grass that claimed it, though overgrown, was greener, as if it had once been tended to. Near the far edge lay a collection of oddly out-of-place boulders. Some of these were cracked and, in places, black scorch marks were visible on them, noticeable only because no mosses or lichens clung to them. The trees closest to the boulders were grey and lifeless.

"This is where I used to practise wielding," said Jon, walking a short way into the glade and looking around. He raised his staff and waved it slowly from side to side. The grass began to rustle then, all at once, fell flat against the ground.

Aldrick was dumbstruck.

"Ah…" he managed, mouth gaping open.

Jon chuckled. "Don't get too excited. The staff is to stay with me," he said, then, noticing Aldrick's continued expression of awe, "it is used to intensify the effects of storm wielding."

"How does it do that?"

"The shaft is fashioned from the wood of the rare lelylan tree. It conducts storm brilliantly. And the gemstone," Jon gestured to the blue oval at the tip of the staff, "is far more efficient at emitting it than our own body. Put the two together and we have a tool that intensifies our powers significantly."

"Awesome."

"Yes, but like I said, you're not getting your hands on it. You're just a beginner, my boy."

"Then show me the way, master," Aldrick joked.

"Very well then."

Jon rested the staff on the ground, stood up and stretched, then paused all of a sudden, like he had just remembered something. "We are ahead of ourselves, Aldrick. You need to understand just what the heck storm is. We have only touched on the subject until now." He scratched his beard and stared down thoughtfully for a time before continuing. "In truth, its nature remains peculiar and elusive. It is believed to be some kind of energy, a life-force which exists in everything... most things. It spills from the heart of this world and flows around every corner of it. If you imagine our sun—always emitting energy," Jon performed some wild gestures with his hands, "well, that is what the heart of the world is believed to do, except the energy emitted is not only heat or light... but storm as well."

"And, so... why do wielders have the ability to control it?" Aldrick asked, bemused. "And how is it that certain things like lelylan wood react to it in unique ways?"

"We believe it has something to do with the physical nature of these things, though the specifics of this theory are unwritten. There is currently research into the elements of physicality being undertaken at Delthendra which may one day shed light on such questions. Until then, we must assume our ability to hold storm within us is a blessing, as are the rare things in this world which improve our ability to wield it."

"Show me how," said Aldrick, feeling a spontaneous spur of confidence. "Show me how to wield magic."

Jon grinned. "Very well." He beckoned Aldrick over to the pile of boulders near the edge of the glade. "Pick one up," he said plainly.

Aldrick stared at him, then down at the boulders. The smallest of them had to be at least twice his weight. "With my hands?"

Jon nodded.

Aldrick reached down, clasped his hands around one of them and tried to heave it from the ground using the strength in his legs. Nothing happened. He tried again. Still nothing. The boulder wasn't going to budge.

"It's impossible," he gasped.

"Ah, but it isn't, Aldrick," Jon said insistently. "You only believe it to be so because you know yourself as a human, not a wielder. You are not aware of the storm within you. You must find it. Make it surge within you. Bring it to the surface and wield it to your purpose."

"How do I find it?"

"By knowing it is there."

"I do know it's there, you've told me so."

"No, I've only made you believe it, not know it."

"Then how do I know it?"

"By finding it."

Aldrick was baffled. "Your meaning isn't clear to me."

"I would not expect it!" Jon exclaimed. "Most wielders spend many years seeking within themselves to find storm. Sadly, many fail to see beyond their own reason. They know they are a wielder, they know storm exists, but they fail to understand their union with it, and therein they lose the ability to truly embrace it. But I believe in you, my boy. I believe you can find faith in who you are, not what you are. That is the key. Achieve this and you will know your storm."

Aldrick squinted, thinking hard upon Jon's words.

"So," he began, "so what I need to find isn't storm, it is faith."

"Yes, Aldrick."

"Faith in myself. I need to... find myself."

Jon nodded.

"Whoa, I haven't talked like this since the last time Kaal and I shared drinks in Rain."

Jon chuckled. "Time well spent," he said, before returning to words of wisdom. "Do you see, Aldrick—the technicalities of the nature of storm—such things are really only valuable as foreknowledge. Find yourself. Know yourself. Only then you will come to realise your powers and your true potential."

Aldrick nodded. He felt Jon's explanation had been rather indirect but reasoned that this had been intentional. There was no straight way to teach something that one can only learn oneself.

"I think I understand," he said. "In my mind I imagined storm as something stored up in a jar somewhere inside me, but now I see it as a part of me... yet, I don't feel any different. I'm still the same old me I have been all my life."

"That is because your storm has always been with you, Aldrick, not letting slip unless your emotions bested your reason, as they did last night."

Aldrick considered this for a moment. Realisation struck him. Last night, it was emotion that surged through him when the skies opened above him. That was a reaction to the anguish inside him. And the day he fell over the cliff with the ka-zchen—those spurring gusts of wind had come just when he needed them, when he feared falling and dying, when he panicked. He had created them.

"But why has my storm *only* made an appearance in those moments?"

"Because it is in those pivotal moments that all the fluff of life and logic disappear and your actions become aligned with your inner self. Storm is then able to flow freely from you and interact with the world around you."

"Then how can wielders control it without being emotionally charged all the time?"

"That comes with time and practise!" cried Jon. "By embracing who they are and coming to know themselves, as I have said. When this is achieved, storm may be wielded at one's leisure. Storm may flow when you are in turmoil, but it floods when you are at peace within yourself. Reaching such a state is a challenge, to be sure, yet it is a fine thing to strive for."

"I see... but you say it can take years? I don't have years to practise, Jon. I have already lost my entire childhood, ignorant to the knowledge of my identity and my past. I don't have time to learn from scratch."

Jon patted him on the shoulder. "I believe in you, my boy." A kind smile lit his face, exercising his many wrinkles.

"You never expected me to be able to lift the boulder, did you?" Aldrick asked.

Jon shook his head. "No, but your effort was not without purpose. I wanted you to question me, to seek your own answers. Besides, you had no idea where to begin. Storm cannot simply increase one's strength.

The technique you needed to apply was 'gravity manipulation', as I did with the grass."

Aldrick's eyebrows rose.

"We can manipulate gravity?" he mouthed. Phelvara had taught him some knowledge of the natural sciences as a child and he recalled learning about forces such as gravity—the worldly pull. As far as he remembered, this was something unchanging, inescapable.

"Indeed we can," said Jon gleefully, delighted by his ability to continually rock the foundations of Aldrick's world. "It is a rudimentary ability all wielders are taught. We can manipulate gravity in ways contrary to its typical downward pull. Observe." He held out one hand toward the boulder, then began to raise it slowly. The boulder trembled a little then, slowly but surely, began to rise into the air. When it was at head height, Jon ceased raising his hand and the boulder simultaneously stopped and levitated there in front of them.

Aldrick stared, amazed and perplexed. "Woah."

Jon relaxed his hand and the boulder fell back to the ground with a loud thud.

"Nicely done!" called out Télia. She was relaxing on the grass with her legs crossed by Jon's staff.

"I concur," said Aldrick, beyond impressed. "May I try?"

"Of course!" cried Jon. "Did you notice how my palm was pointed toward the boulder while I raised it? That is where we are able to naturally emit the most storm from our body. With two hands holding it as you did before, you won't have to radiate your storm as far and should have less difficulty focusing on raising the boulder alone. I suggest you continue using such an approach."

"Right." Aldrick marched up to the boulder. "So I must know myself, that it is within my power to lift it?"

"Yes, focus only on yourself wanting to do so, and then on the act of lifting it as a secondary thing, because you already know you are capable of that."

Aldrick rubbed his hands together.

"Lift it with gravity... I can do that," he told himself. "I think," he added.

Again he bent down and pressed his palms firmly against the rough surface of the boulder. He wanted to lift it, he knew he could. He visualised it rising upward, then heaved with every ounce of might he could muster. Nothing happened. The boulder didn't even tremble as it had before Jon lifted it.

Aldrick gave up and slumped down with his back against the boulder. "It's no use, Jon. I can't do this."

"You will come to learn," said Jon calmly. "No wielder, nor will any wielder, ever be able to achieve such a thing on their first day attempting it."

For a time Aldrick didn't move. A faint ache in his head had become a heavy throb and his left shoulder felt freshly strained. He closed his eyes. In the background he heard footsteps as Télia walked through the glade. She began to converse with Jon but Aldrick paid no attention to their words. Instead he thought of the past and of the future. He wanted the ones responsible for murdering his parents to meet justice. The wielder Malath must have his life taken from him. It was his crime. He may have evaded reckoning all these years, but for no longer.

Aldrick's mind wandered to his family in the south. They were dearly missed. He hoped Braem had found Phelvara and his siblings safe in Rain, that none of this would affect them any more than it already had. It wasn't their problem to face. Every memory of them he cherished. Still, it was infuriating that the life he would have lived was robbed of him. He needed to master control of his stormpowers—his mother's one—her ability to take storm from another. That was how he would defeat Malath. Perhaps they did need the Halfstone Jon had spoken of, but either way, he wished to come face to face with Malath. The prospect didn't ignite any fear in him, not as the mere mentioning of the wielder's name had in Télia. Perhaps this was because he had never known of Malath's wickedness. There was much he remained ignorant of.

"Do you wish to continue, Aldrick?" Jon's voice broke his trail of thoughts.

He got to his feet and rubbed his shoulder. "I do, I want to. I want to learn my mother's ability. Can you teach me that?"

Jon surveyed Aldrick from beneath his bushy, white eyebrows.

"I can only guide you in learning it yourself," he said. "It may be more dangerous than the practice of common abilities. You will need to practise on me directly for only I possess storm for you to take."

"Maybe it is unsafe then," Aldrick said with dwindling confidence.

"Well yes," agreed Jon, "Yet it is crucial. What you must first do, though, is spend more time practising what I have already endeavoured to teach."

"Very well."

"It is the only way. Know yourself, Aldrick. Know your intent. Focus. Let your storm be heard."

Aldrick practised for a further hour under Jon's supervision. Jon offered no further instruction beyond that point though, encouraging him go on without distraction. He had surrendered any attempt to physically lift the boulder. Instead he heeded Jon's words and searched for the faith to will it to do so with his storm. He willed it to rise from the earth. He told himself he could make it do so with every attempt, yet the boulder remained stubbornly motionless. Eventually frustration and annoyance bested him and he gave up.

Jon and Télia were relaxing at the edge of the glade. The position of the sun told him it was past noon already. He was exhausted and wanted water.

"I'm going for a break," he said, making for the track.

"We are right behind you," Jon said, rising to his feet. Télia aided him. Though very subtle, there were signs that age was taking its toll on his body.

Back at the house the three shared refreshments and took advantage of the cool indoor air.

"It's just not coming to me, Jon," Aldrick said grumpily from an armchair.

"Because it must come *from* you," replied Jon adamantly. "Maybe try to find a reason—a motive to accomplish your goal."

Aldrick contemplated this. He did have a motive—to become powerful enough to avenge his parents. Perhaps this was too vague. He needed inspiration.

"You could try practicing alone next time—allow yourself some peace," suggested Télia. She sat in one corner of the room polishing her crossbow.

Jon stopped rummaging in a kitchen cupboard and looked up at her. "A wise idea. You are an astute aera for your age, my dear."

Télia looked both flattered and offended.

"Right then, I'm off," Aldrick said, having found enough motivation to heave himself to his feet.

"I'm off for a while too," said Télia, also standing. "I'm going to take De'ama for a walk and explore the area."

"Very well, you two leave and I shall remain here," said Jon. "I have much to think upon and there is no place like the comfort of one's solitary mind to do such a thing."

Aldrick and Télia left together but parted ways at the stables.

"I believe you can do anything you set your mind to, Aldrick," Télia shouted out as he entered the forest.

He looked back and smiled. She stood aside her mare, returning one. He was comforted knowing she was near. She was so, *so* incredibly beautiful, and yet so dangerous, like a goddess from a mystical fable, a guardian angel sent to protect him. His smile lingered all the way to the glade. A peaceful sense of solitude welcomed him back. For a fleeting moment it felt as though he was back in the forests of the Mountains Rain, far from the concerns of the surrounding world. Here, though, storm had left its mark; the grass remained flattened and the boulders misplaced. He walked up to them with his hands in his pockets. He didn't feel like beginning immediately and instead closed his eyes and enjoyed the calming silence.

The sudden fluttering of wings caught his attention. He opened his eyes to see a black fantail staring back at him, its head cocked to one side. The bird had perched on the outreaching branch of one of the lifeless trees. With a single chirp it flew away again, into the forest. Aldrick watched it go. On the ground, beneath where it disappeared between the branches, he noticed a path which led up in the direction of the mountain tops. It was long overgrown but very definitely a path. Either Jon had made it or some animal seeking to graze in the glade. Curious, he decided to follow it. The path led him through dense undergrowth up to the treeline, whereupon it veered right. He continued along it until he found himself at the edge of a small tarn that hid within flowing golden grass. The water was crystal clear. At the base of the tarn, a smooth bowl of white clay reflected the sun's brilliant light. A breeze swept across the surface of the water that shadows mimed in a dance upon the clay.

Glancing across to the far side of the tarn, Aldrick's eyes fell upon a small area where an assortment of flowering plants grew. Nestled within them was some kind of small stone statue. He made his way around to it. It appeared to be the headstone of a grave. He squinted down at small letters etched into the stone. His heart stopped. It read 'Isobel Clarice Aedimon'. This was where Jon had buried his mother.

7

ALLIES

A ldrick stood before his mother's grave. The initial shock of reading her name upon the headstone had subsided, giving way to an unexpected sense of clarity. He didn't feel sadness or anger, not resentment for past events nor bitterness to bear with him in future ones. He was grounded. Here his mother lay, at his feet, forging a vivid connection between him and the fantasy world which had been unveiled around him. He found himself. He knew who he was.

The flowers adorning the grave were in full bloom even though their season had come and gone many months ago. It was a sign that Isobel was here with him, that Gilthred was too. They had never intended to leave him in this world alone. They hadn't; their storm was invested in him. It was his to wield now.

He stooped, plucked a single blue orchid and rested it on top of the headstone. His hand lingered there for a moment then he turned and retraced the path back into the forest. When he re-entered the glade he strode purposefully toward the boulders but stopped before reaching them. He outstretched his arm, directed his palm toward the surface of one and closed his eyes. Slowly, he began to raise his hand. He felt the gravity holding the boulder to the ground wane as he willed it upward using his own gravitational push. He could feel the boulder, like it was trying to resist, but he would not let it. He opened his eyes. There it was, levitating in front of him. His focus faltered and it began to fall, though at an unnaturally slow speed, back to the ground.

"No!" He would not let his achievement be so brief. Again he raised his hand. The boulder rose in turn. He cast it sideways and it hurtled into the trunk of one of the dead trees. There was a mighty smash as solid stone met feeble wood and the tree collapsed. The boulder met ground a short way beyond it and rolled to a halt at the base of another tree. Aldrick remained standing, arm outstretched, ogling at what he had done. He took a series of long, deep breaths. He could do it! He could wield! He had power. It felt good.

There were hurried footsteps behind him. Jon burst into the glade with his staff clenched in his hand. "Aldrick! Aldrick, wha…" His attention fell upon the felled tree and the absence of the boulder. He relaxed. "Ah, I had feared the worst, but it appears that clamour was of your making."

"Jon, I did it!" Aldrick exclaimed. "I threw the boulder into the tree!"

"So I see." Jon came to his side. "Truly incredible. I am most impressed, my boy."

Télia appeared. She wore an expression more of excitement than concern. "I felt your storm surge, Aldrick. Have you done it? Have you wielded your storm?"

"Yes," he said, now trying to sound as casual as possible.

The wide smile he adored so much lit Télia's face. "That's brilliant news. Well done!" She turned and looked at Jon incredulously. "So much for no wielder being able to achieve such a thing on their first day of training."

"Well I..." Jon began, searching for words. "It's unheard of, until today. Young Aldrick here will become a wielder of the highest calibre, to be sure."

Excitement welled inside Aldrick. He could truly wield! He had found his storm. He yearned to do more. "Are there further abilities you can teach me, Jon?"

"Indeed. There is much more I can show you."

"Then let's begin."

Jon chuckled. "I remember being in your shoes, Aldrick. The first time I successfully wielded, all I wanted to do was to do it more. It is a marvellous thing, having such power."

"Don't let it go to your head," said Télia.

Though she spoke light-heartedly, Aldrick could tell her advice was sincere. He imagined she had experienced the arrogance of wielders. Jon appeared to be level headed, though. He was glad of that.

"Télia's words are wisdom," said Jon. "It is rare to find a modest wielder. It is a consequence of the core principle of wielding being the focus on one's self. It is bad for anyone to do that too often."

"Were my parents arrogant wielders?" Aldrick asked, considering how little he knew about them.

"Your father, a little," Jon said contemplatively. "Your mother was quite the selfless one, though."

"As you are, Jon," said Télia warmly.

Jon almost looked embarrassed. "Yes, well, in my life I have found my concerns turned outward, toward other people."

"That is an admirable thing, just so long as you are first at ease with yourself."

"Yes," Aldrick agreed, endeavouring for Télia's favour.

Jon left them and walked to the edge of the glade, where he paused in front of a low-hanging branch.

"Aldrick, come," he beckoned. "You wished to learn more, did you not? Well, I will show you something quite constructive us wielders can do... if done under the right circumstances, of course." He held up a part of the branch that appeared to have been snapped recently. The leaves still had hints of green.

Aldrick peered at it. "What are you going to do?"

Jon didn't answer. He raised his free hand and held it over the branch. For a moment nothing happened then, slowly, the leaves turned greener, blending back in with the rest of the tree.

Aldrick was astounded. "You're... you're healing it."

"Yes—a little miracle we can perform," said Jon, admiring his handiwork. "It is an ability often overshadowed by the more grandiose ones we are known to perform. It can also be used to heal injuries, of sorts."

"How do I wield it?"

"By focusing on your will to do good, Aldrick. It is the true test of a wielder's heart. Someone like Malath would struggle with such an ability even if they cared greatly for what it was they wanted to heal, simply because they do not bear a nurturing heart. But you, my boy, I am certain you have more than just your mother's eyes."

Aldrick searched for another dying branch to practise on but couldn't find one. The rest of the tree was healthy.

"Aldrick, I have a bruise on my knee from the brawl at the inn," said Télia, coming to him. "Perhaps you could heal that for me."

As much as he liked the idea, he was hesitant. "Might it be unsafe for me to focus my storm upon someone just yet?"

Jon shrugged. "If Télia wishes it then I hold no concern. You have already shown unprecedented ability. I trust you will do her no harm."

"So, will you?" Télia challenged.

"Very well, I will."

She sat on the ground, lay her crossbow beside her, then rolled up her earth-brown trousers to just above her knee. On her knee was a dull purple and yellow bruise where it had struck the inn floor. Aldrick knelt by her and placed his palm over the bruise. He wanted to be sure he focused on the injured area alone.

"Are you ready?" he asked nervously.

Télia stared straight into him. "Are you?"

Her intimate presence was fogging his mind and reddening his cheeks, but he tried his best to keep his focus. He shut his eyes and let his mind rest on his desire to make her knee well again. For a time it seemed as though he was achieving nothing, but then he felt an increase in warmth beneath his hand. Télia's leg flinched. Aldrick pulled his hand away fearing he had hurt her, but found that the bruise had all but disappeared. The area was now as impeccably smooth and toned as the rest of her skin.

"Thank you," she said, rolling her trouser leg back down.

"What did it feel like?" he asked.

"A little ticklish. I have never had a wielder as a healer before."

"I have never had an aera as a patient."

"How did it go?" called out Jon. He had left to inspect the toppled tree.

"Well," said Télia brightly. "I think Aldrick is ready to practise more trying incantations, Jon."

"That may well be so, but I wager he is in need of another break first. Wielding quickly exhausts a novice's energy."

Aldrick did feel the need to rest again. He was tired and hungry, as if he had been exercising both his mind and body for hours.

The three of them made their way back to the house.

De'ama greeted Télia with a soft neigh at the entrance to the forest, where she had been patiently awaiting her return. It was now mid-afternoon and there was little that begged attention indoors. Jon charmed Télia into the kitchen to teach her how to make his self-proclaimed 'finest bread in the Narathlands'. Aldrick sat in his own company on the doorstep with a mug of milk. Around him, the green and gold landscape bathed in sunlight. The sky was a calm ocean of blue. There was so much beauty to behold in the world, he thought. It saddened him that his parents weren't here to enjoy it. Their lives had been cut short in the pursuit of justice. The time to pursue vengeance was drawing ever closer. He waited until Jon and Télia had left their bread dough to rise, then rekindled the conversation which had been pending since last night.

"Since last night my mind has remained clear to me," he began. "I'm going to go after Malath Jayther. He has done wrongs that I cannot ignore. It's clear that he wants me dead too. That means I threaten him. I was born with an advantage and there are means by which it can be used to be rid of him. I need the stone my parents found—the Halfstone. If it is truly vital in assuring his defeat then I'm going to find it. What I wonder, though, is if I will have some company on this venture?"

He looked at them both. Jon was seated with his arms crossed, deep in thought. Télia leant against the wall, watching him closely.

"I will be at your side, Aldrick," she said. "Not only because I have been entrusted with doing so, but because I believe in you. It is a path you are meant to take."

He smiled at her.

"Of course I will aid you too, my boy," said Jon, standing. He came and rested his hands on Aldrick's shoulders. "We share motive."

Then it was settled. They were taking matters into their own hands. They were going to take on Malath.

"I appreciate having you both at my side," Aldrick said with gratification. "You have already helped me a lot and knowing you'll remain close…" Emotion washed through him. It was a huge undertaking he had proposed and he found great comfort in their willingness to take it with him.

He gathered himself. "Where do we go from here? Where is the Halfstone now?"

"In Fort Blackbed, I presume," said Jon. "We must visit that dark place. There is a fine chance that is also where we will encounter Malath and Selayna."

"Now if only we had the Synod's support for this venture," Télia huffed. "The reinforcements they said they were sending to protect Aldrick never arrived."

"Reinforcements?" questioned Jon.

"Yes. They were supposed to be sending more aeras."

"And you have had no further word on this?"

"No…"

Jon began to pace.

"Worrying, to say the least," he muttered. "We must hope there is a simple explanation for their absence."

"You don't think Malath has something to do with

it, do you?" Télia asked nervously.

Jon scratched his cheek. "I cannot say, but assumedly the Synod knew of Malath's return to power when they repurposed you to be Aldrick's aera. It is not impossible that there has since been a confrontation with him."

"By confrontation you mean battle?"

"I suppose so, yes." Jon frowned. "I had not expected Malath to be quite so bold."

Télia turned away in distress.

"Then we must act now!" she cried. "If Malath has already invaded Galdrem who knows how close he may be to accessing the Shard of Heart's Storm. We may already be too late!"

"Yes, we should leave soon. Finding the Halfstone could take more time than we have," said Aldrick, sharing Télia's concern.

Jon nodded. "Indeed. We will make way at the break of dawn tomorrow and hope that time is our ally. Even if Malath is in Galdrem, I am willing to wager that the Halfstone remains in Blackbed, in safe keeping. He would not carry such a haunting trinket on him. We have dwindling time to ready ourselves for this journey. You must practise your mother's ability with me shortly, Aldrick. It is most important."

"I'll meet you outside?"

"Yes, but eat first and rest a little while longer. I imagine you are still weakened from your previous practise. I will see to some travel necessities in the meantime." Jon left for his study.

Aldrick went to the kitchen to find food. Télia

followed him.

"I am wary of all this, Aldrick," she said, standing by him. "What if we are too late? What if our efforts prove hopeless? We are but three souls against unfathomably wicked ones."

Aldrick bit his lip. "We may be too late, but however late we are, I will see Malath to his grave."

Télia smiled. "Your passion is strong. I'm glad to see it hasn't clouded reason. Going after the Halfstone is the best course of action. To confront Malath without such a thing... would not end well."

"Well, we had better hope we find it then."

"We can always hope, but if we don't find it, just remember Aldrick—there is always a path to achieve that which you desire, however unlikely or obscure it might seem."

Her words were calming but he wondered if they held as much truth as intended reassurance.

"I hope you are right," he said.

"Concentrate!" cried Jon in frustration. "You have shown me what you are capable of. Now, prove yourself further and take my storm from me!"

Aldrick wiped his brow. The falling sun was still hot and he too was losing patience. He raised his hand once more, palm directed toward Jon's chest. He focused as intently as he was able, willing Jon's storm to come to him. Jon's staff continued to levitate above his hand—evidence his storm remained within him.

"It's no use. I can't do it," Aldrick huffed, kicking

the ground irately. "The other abilities—those were clearer to me."

Jon sighed and the staff returned to his hand. "Perhaps there is something we haven't touched on, Aldrick." He frowned thoughtfully for a moment before raising a finger. "The nature of Isobel's ability... the unique motivation behind it. We must take that into our considerations."

"Self-preservation, perhaps?" Aldrick suggested.

Jon pondered. "Mmm yes, I suppose—self-preservation in the presence of one who means to inflict harm. Perhaps you cannot take my storm from me because I am not your foe, Aldrick."

"Well how do we get around that?" he asked. "We can't go seeking out danger just to practise."

"No," agreed Jon. "Which is why I must reiterate that, for the time being, focus is the key—to truly envisage your need to wield the power and to master the belief that you can."

"Very well."

Aldrick tried many further times to drain Jon's storm, but to no success. Eventually they both had spent their patience and returned to the house to finish preparing for the journey the coming day. They entered to find Télia with all her gear packed and ready to be loaded on her mare in the morning.

"You ready yourself with purpose, my dear," commented Jon.

"Action spurred by concern," she replied restlessly.

Jon took her hands. "No doubt this is a great undertaking for you, Télia—following your wielder into the shadows like this. It is a noble thing for an aera only in training to do. I am most thankful to have you here and to know you stand at Aldrick's side."

Télia didn't reply but offered Jon a faint smile and nod of appreciation. Aldrick was also sincerely grateful for her willingness to take part in this quest. Anyone else might have fled in the opposite direction, but not her. She bore a courageous spirit and a caring heart.

The faint but undeniable rumble of hooves came into earshot. Like lightning Télia went for her crossbow. Jon summoned his staff to hand. Aldrick clambered for his bow and readied it with an arrow.

"This may well be trouble!" cried Jon in alarm.

Télia made for the door. "Come, we mustn't find ourselves trapped in here!"

They ran at great pace into the nearby forest and hid behind some leafy undergrowth.

"Keep ready," Télia whispered. "If one is an aera they will sense you two are here."

Aldrick stealthily drew his arrow, and a breath. They were probably more assassins under Selayna's command. It was best they be killed before they had a chance to attack. By the sound of the hooves he judged there were another two of them.

After a moment of tremendous tension, the riders came swiftly into sight, galloping up the track toward Jon's house. They wore dark green cloaks. Outside the house they came to an abrupt halt, dismounted and drew crossbows from their saddle bags. As Télia had feared, their attention did not fall on the house, but on the area of forest in which the three of them hid.

Aldrick felt his heart start to thump...

"Wait." Télia grabbed his drawing arm. "I know who they are!" she exclaimed excitedly. "They are aeras from Galdrem. They are our allies!"

He and Jon stared at her.

"Are you certain?" asked Jon hesitantly.

Télia lowered her crossbow. "Yes, I am certain." She stepped out from the trees and walked toward the new arrivals. "Sinin!" she called out.

One of the riders—a bearded man with long hair—held up a hand in recognition. "Télia. Télia, you are here."

"Indeed," she said brightly. "In the company of my wielder, and another." She gestured to Aldrick and Jon's position behind her. They exchanged looks, then cautiously made their way out from the trees.

Télia met Sinin with a lengthy embrace, as she had shared with Aldrick when they first met, then turned. "Aldrick, Jon, this is Sinin, an old friend from the aera's lodge in Galdrem."

Jon strode to Sinin and greeted him with the same warm embrace. "Another aera? Well, it is my pleasure. I welcome you and your companion to my humble home."

"It is a pleasure to be here," Sinin replied kindly. "I come with a fellow aera, Aru," he gestured to the woman he rode with, "to aid in the protection of the young wielder."

"My name is Aldrick," he remarked, offering Sinin a handshake then greeting Aru in turn. He was grumpy. Télia was not meant to have a man friend who was ruggedly handsome and some years older than her. Still, it was heartening to be welcoming allies into their company.

"How did you find us here?" Télia asked the newcomers while they walked their horses to the stable.

"As any aeras worth their guts would have," replied Sinin. "We asked the right questions of the right people and learnt of your last known path very easily.

"Too easily," protested Aru, speaking for the first time. Her arms were crossed and she wore a firm frown. "Enemies could find you here at any time."

"We have been on guard," Télia said defensively. "Besides, we intend to leave from here in short time."

"Indeed we do," affirmed Jon. "There are most pressing concerns we must discuss."

Sinin stopped walking and ran a hand through his hair. "I fear we arrive here in the wake of dire circumstances, likely of the nature you are concerned about."

"What do you speak of?" asked Jon nervously.

"Malath Jayther and his faithful have come to the north. They set upon Galdrem days ago," said Aru.

"No," uttered Télia in a voice stifled by dismay. The usual warm tones of her face faded and were replaced by those of a morn frost.

"It is true, I fear," said Sinin grimly. "Our journey to you was delayed because of this. Malath's power has returned and he is using it to hold the Synod by the neck. The city is in anarchy. We were told to find Aldrick a week ago but that same day Malath strode up the front steps of the high council building and declared lordship of the city and lands. As you can imagine, the Synod had a thing or two to say about that. Battle broke out. There have already been casualties. It's not pretty."

Jon's head dropped. "The worst of our fears are realised then. Malath already moves to fulfil his old and dark desires, and there are few standing in his way who threaten him."

"Fewer now," said Aru. "Half of the wielders in Galdrem are unaccounted for."

"What of Devéna?" Jon queried anxiously.

"I cannot say. We heard that a number of wielders are held up in the Synod's sanctuary. Malath was unable to break through the warding enchantments placed upon it. Devéna may be among the survivors."

"So there is some good news."

"Some," said Sinin. "Though I fear how this may end. Malath has taken Delthendra as his own and given the Synod only days from now to declare their allegiance to him. If they refuse he will make efforts to take these lands by way of annihilation. He threatens to obtain the Shard of Heart's Storm."

"We three were wary of such intent," said Jon, trading glances with Aldrick and Télia. "Malath will try to get the Shard whether the Synod kiss his boots or not. Fortunately, we may still have time. He won't find opening the holding chamber any simple task."

"I wouldn't be so sure of that. He uttered troubling words, Jon. He said red wings will descend upon Darkna."

Jon stared at Sinin for a moment then turned, twisting his lip.

"Oh dear me," he remarked. "This is far worse than bad. Come—see your horses to comfort and then we shall speak more of this indoors."

Red wings? Aldrick thought to himself. What could that mean?

Once inside, Jon offered their two new companions food and water. They then seated themselves in a rough circle so as to hear and share each other's thoughts. Télia sat next to Aldrick. He could sense her unease. Her home village, Daraki' Anya, was close to Galdrem. It may have already suffered in the wake of Malath's return.

He rested a hand on her shoulder.

"We are going to fix all this," he said as tenderly as he could. He wasn't sure what else to say.

Télia didn't offer a response, just continued to stare blankly forward.

"Well now, let us talk." Jon sat with his legs crossed and hands on his knees. He glanced steadily around at each of them. "Firstly, let us talk about dragons. It sounds as though we may have to add one to our list of foes."

What! Dragons? … Dragons?! Surely Aldrick had misheard.

Télia stared at Jon with widened eyes. "No… they don't exist, not in this age."

Jon shook his head. "Now Malath possesses his storm again there is little from the past he cannot bring back to haunt this world. His foul sister was just the beginning, I fear."

"It is a certainty that 'red wings' referred to a dragon," said Aru. "There have been reports from a village near Mur that the gorge was recently visited by a company of riders. It is the only known location where the remains of a dragon lie. Malath plans to return it to life, has he not already."

Jon nodded. "It is the likely truth. His wielding ability will be as strong as ever, possibly even more so given the years he has spent disempowered and resentful of his fate. If he gets his hands on the Shard there will truly be carnage as has not been seen in a thousand years."

"And I hear this lad is our only hope," said Sinin, turning his attention to Aldrick.

Jon shot Aldrick a quick glance.

"That may be so, though it is not nearly that simple," he said. "We seek to obtain the stone which trapped Malath's powers many years ago, to ensure victory over him this time. Without it in Aldrick's possession, his chances are infinitesimal at best."

Sinin nodded musingly. "It would seem you are steps ahead of us then. We came with no plan of retaliation."

"Yet you can provide invaluable support of our own," said Télia. "Tomorrow we travel for Selayna's old Blackbed hideout, where we hope to find the stone. It is the likeliest place Malath has kept it hidden from the world all these years."

Sinin's eyebrows rose. "A bold move... but spurred by sound reasoning it would seem. Aru and I will gladly accompany you. After all, it is our job to protect Aldrick."

Jon clapped his hands together. "It is most excellent to have you on board. The extra arms you offer mean I shall be more willing to part from this venture."

Aldrick looked up. "What? You aren't coming with us?"

Jon looked at him with reluctance in his eyes. "For some of the way I shall, but I must make way to Galdrem. If the Synod has been given only days to surrender, which they will not, then I must be there to protect the Shard of Heart's Storm, and the peoples of the Narathlands, just as I once swore to. It is my duty, one I have abandoned for far too long."

His words were disheartening. The knowledge that a powerful wielder would accompany him to Fort Blackbed had been a large part of Aldrick's motivation to go there. Now it felt only perilous and foolhardy.

"Do not fret, my boy" said Jon, sensing his disappointment. "You will find your way. With Malath in Galdrem, it is likely that the fort will be ill-guarded."

Télia nudged his shoulder. "You'll still have us aeras at your side."

Aldrick smiled and looked around at the three of them.

"I am grateful for it," he said. "But know that I want none of you to protect me any more than you would each other. I invite the support of willing companions, not bodyguards."

Sinin chuckled. "These words I endorse. What real man needs us three watching his back? You are a real man, are you not, Aldrick?

"No, I am a wielder," he replied.

"Like father, like son," Jon said fondly. "So it is settled. Tomorrow we shall leave here. Our cause is the same, though we have our own parts to play and paths to follow. Let us pray, to whatever ethereal beings may be listening, that this all ends well."

"It had better," said Sinin, rising. "But in case it does not, let us celebrate now and die later. Jon, do you have drink?"

"You have your priorities in order, my friend," Jon said with elevating spirits. "The answer is yes, I do. Let me fetch us some wine. We must share mugs!"

They did indeed share mugs. Jon retrieved enough dusty wine bottles from a small cellar to supply a tavern for a week, many of which were hastily claimed by Sinin who proceeded to down them as if his life depended on it. Aldrick also found himself drinking more than he judged to be wise. It was a fine wine, made from the merry grape—a rare berry found only in the eastern provinces, Jon had proudly told him. Télia expressed her appreciation of it, but drank sparingly, instead spending time in the kitchen preparing food. She insisted that they must fill their stomachs.

"We have an early start and a long journey ahead of us, my friends," she said, resisting Sinin's attempt to claim her as a dance partner.

Jon was by the fire playing a jolly tune on a flute and dancing with Aru. It was a peculiar dance with lots of small jumps and spinning that Aldrick had never seen before, but then again, he had never been much of a dancer.

Aru appeared to be enjoying herself, though like Télia, she had refrained from consuming much wine. She was smiling, unlike upon her arrival. Second to Jon, she was the oldest among them. Her face bore the permanent markings of many trying days—serving in conflicts under the command of the Synod, Aldrick supposed.

He had chosen to distance himself from the dancing and stood near the kitchen, separated from Télia by the bench. He used it to rest an elbow on while he drank.

"Are you feeling all right?" Télia asked, catching him staring down into his mug.

"I'm fine thanks," he replied. "I was just considering that I should probably put my drink down and keep my mind afloat. There is nothing worse than waking to a throbbing headache."

Télia laughed. "I have had my fair share of such mornings, which is why I cautioned you all. We need to keep our wits about us. There could be danger at any time, even tonight."

"Let your guard down, Télia, there will be no danger tonight. Be merry!" Sinin had overheard them talking while he clumsily refilled his two mugs.

Télia sighed. "Fine, but I will not drink like you. I intend to preserve my dignity."

Sinin bowed.

"Princess," he said, then returned to dance with the others.

Télia's mood did brighten after that point. With

Aldrick's help, she served a sumptuous dinner of goat meat and fresh vegetables from Jon's garden. The smells quickly drew the others to the kitchen bench.

"Simply delicious!" exclaimed Jon, sampling the vegetables. "What herbs did you use, dear?"

Télia shrugged. "Just a whole lot. In Daraki, everyone loves cooking. My grandmother taught me all the secrets of making vegetables the tastiest part of a meal. It is a trick she used on me as a child."

Jon chuckled. Aldrick was glad the mood was light. It was what they needed. Beyond tonight there was no knowing when they would next have time to unwind and enjoy each other's company. Moments such as this affirmed to him that they were doing the right thing. It was not reckless going after Malath, nor was it heroic. It was simply just.

At a late hour, after they had filled their stomachs to excess, they found themselves collapsed on and around the seating area, with the flames of the fire ever faithfully providing warmth and soothing light. The food seemed to have dulled the effects the wine had on Jon and he now rekindled talk of the journey ahead.

"We will follow the valley path as far north as convenient then make way across the Lonely Province," he said. "When we reach Old Capital Road I will follow it to Galdrem. You four will continue on into the Blackbed Plains. The fort won't be difficult to find. It burrows into a solitary mountain in the north."

"So, first the Lonely Province and then the Blackbed Plains? Both those places sound awfully cheery," Aldrick remarked.

"The Lonely Province inherited its name after Prithe fell. Since then it has been all but deserted. It is a land of forgotten beauty. Blackbed, on the other hand... you will know that place when you see it, Aldrick."

Sinin yawned and rubbed his eyes. "Right now I wish only to know the comfort of a soft surface beneath me."

Jon rose. "Yes, it is indeed time for us to rest." He bid them goodnight and made his way upstairs to bed.

Sinin and Aru claimed the area by the fire. They had brought their own sleeping gear. While they settled down, Télia beckoned Aldrick to her room. He went gladly.

"Sleep on the floor in here," she said, handing him her spare pillow.

"All right," he said, hiding his disappointment. Spending another night in the same bed as her was perhaps a little too much to ask.

Télia glanced into the living room then spoke in a whisper. "It may seem silly to you but I was taught never to trust one whom I don't know or know of. I won't have you sleeping in the same room as Aru."

He was puzzled by this. Wasn't Aru also an aera, entrusted to protect him? She might not be the most polite person in the world, but was there really any reason to distrust her? He let it go. He was happy to once more spend a night in Télia's close company, hopefully not to be interrupted by any visitors of ill-will this time.

They spoke no more. As they lay in silence there was much on their minds. Their fates were uncertain.

Come the morning light, they would set out toward dark and dreadful things.

8

DARK AND DREADFUL THINGS

Flame was absent from the many candles that lined the walls. Malath preferred it this way. He felt a resonant sense of seclusion within the shadows. Behind him the statue of Akimr, The First Wielder, stood, headless and scorched by the heat of stormfire. It was a befitting state. Akimr had once made a deplorable choice—to embrace a life amongst the putrid and stifling human race. They were empty vessels, all of them. They possessed no storm, no higher purpose and no desire for one. It was he, Malath, the almighty one, who had come to his senses and seen that the only way toward an enlightened world was to first see humankind extinguished from it. The long years he had spent cursed to be as one of them had not swayed him from his will to turn old desires into reality. The time was growing near when he would have unspeakable power and the ability to make them so. Galdrem quivered at his feet. The remnants of the Synod were trapped, cowering in a corner behind a feeble warding enchantment. He could crush the life from them if he did so desire, yet he retained hope that they would see the light and join him, that they would stand with him when the time of the cleansing came. The very thought of the cleansing made him shudder with anticipation and pleasure.

He rose and took a long, deep breath of the stagnant air. The smells of fire and blood lingered. He closed his eyes and summoned two souls from the somnolent world of the Life Afterwards to his presence. Slowly, they appeared like twilight mist—pallid reflections of their demised physical counterparts. One was a vast figure that engulfed much of the hall and, without confinement, disappeared beyond the stone walls. It was curled up in a slumber—a colossal mound of ridged stone, a dormant volcano. The other levitated before him, staring at him through dark, sinister eyes—a simple, stout figure, just as Malath remembered him.

"My lord?" The figure spoke in a distant, echoing voice. "My lord, it is my honour to be summoned before you."

Malath placed a hand over his heart. He was humbled by those words. "Dron, your allegiance never fades, not even in death. Soon, though, you will be back at my side. At this very moment my servants seek out your burial chamber. I shall bind you to your bones and you will walk in this world once more."

Dron rubbed his hands together. "I yearn for that day, my lord, and I lust for vengeance on those who took my life."

"You will have it, Dron, as I shall see my own endeavour complete." He gestured to the massive soul beyond him. "That is Aashkara, a dragon of old. I shall resurrect her also. She is to help me gain access to the Shard of Heart's Storm. No enchantment will withstand her fury."

Dron gaped at the dragon's soul.

"A fearsome beast to behold!" he exclaimed. "With her allegiance victory is all but fated."

"Oh yes, none now stand in my way. There were murmurings of some bastard offspring of my defiler, but my sweet sister sent servants to end him."

"Good. Very good."

A deep, menacing grumble began that echoed around the hall and sent tremors through the floor. Aashkara opened her lizard eyes and raised her head. "Storm wielder, my longing to fly with air beneath my wings grows difficult to bear." Her cavernous tones exuded might and ferocity.

Malath stood his ground. He needed to appear steady in the wake of such immense power. "You shall be able to very soon, Aashkara. I swear it to you."

"Yes, I shall." She closed her eyes again and rested her head. "I await my resurrection. Do not prolong it or else when I awaken you will find my temper... unruly."

"Very well." Malath released Aashkara's soul back to the Life Afterwards. Her ghostly form dissipated into the shadows like thinning smoke.

"Do you trust the dragon?" Dron asked. "She is a force not to be reckoned with."

"Oh, she will do exactly as I say," Malath said confidently. "We have already reached an agreement. One she will not retreat from."

"Why is that?"

"She believes in forgotten myths. She believes that if she destroys Darkna her kin will be freed from eternal damnation."

Dron nodded. "Ah, I see. Very cunning. You are very much your old self, my lord."

"As you shall be your old self soon, Storm Brother."

Dron bowed his head low. At a wave of Malath's hand, he faded away.

Alone again, Malath began to laugh. His dream was soon to be fulfilled. He would have lordship over these lands, and perhaps one day those beyond the horizon too!

He heard footsteps and spun around. A silhouette appeared at the far end of the hall which sparked anger in him. "Sister, why have you not left from this place? Did I not request you to oversee preparations for the resurrection?"

Selayna approached him with a lofty step. Candles sprung to life around her, illuminating her figure. Her drathen-blue dress flowed like a flame in a breeze. "Dear Brother, the task you set me upon was indeed important, but it needed not my personal attention. I sent some faithful in my stead. I remained here, to have a little fun." She took a carving knife from her belt and brandished it before her. It was stained with blood.

Malath's frown lingered for a moment longer before

he relaxed. "Well then, I see you have done no wrong." He seated himself. "Now tell me, Sister, just what wickedness have you been up to? Why do you bear such an obsolete weapon?"

Selayna twisted her face into a cheeky sneer. "I've been using this knife of late for I have realised humans simply cannot comprehend my powers. They know not what our storm can do to them, Brother. But this little knife—they know exactly what it can do and when they feel it sever their flesh, the pain they feel... it is more real to them. That makes inflicting it all the more enjoyable. They writhe and squeal like little piglets."

Malath chuckled. "Your macabre tendencies worry me. I fear your mind hangs from but a thread."

"Nonsense!" she snapped. "My mind is well intact. I but bleed animals, soon to go to the slaughter anyway, and that will be your doing, not mine."

"Indeed it will." He stood up. "Have you pictured it, Sister? Thousands of Sanswords arisen, my word their will. Cities will fall at their feet. The people will decay to bones, and we... we will stand and watch it befall." He grasped his sister's hand and stared into her widened eyes. "We will stand as the gods of this world."

She gasped. "We will, won't we?" Her eyes welled with tears. "Oh Brother, words still fail me. You are my saviour. All those years in death, my soul was tortured with the deepest despair. All I wanted was to be back at your side. You granted me that wish and brought me back, and now, now you offer up the world. I thought that dream long lost." She buried her head in his robes and sobbed uncontrollably.

Malath held her close to him. "Sister, do not fret. Nothing is lost. I know with absolute certainty that I shall never lose you again, for the day I die we shall go forth into the Life Afterwards, together." He kissed her softly on the forehead. She raised her head and stared up at him through wisps of damp hair. He felt warmth in his heart. He loved her dearly. It had nearly destroyed him when she was killed. Seeking revenge had offered little solace. That he might one day be able to return her to this world was the hope that had seen him through these past decades. The cleansing would be unfulfilling without her close, irreplaceable comfort.

He guided Selayna to her feet and took her hands in his own. "Go now and see yourself well attended. Mingle with our kinfolk. Spend no more time with those who are damned."

She wiped tears from her eyes and smiled weakly.

"As you wish," she stammered, then hurried from the hall.

It was silent once more. Malath stood, now not quite knowing what to do with himself. He was comfortable within the confines of his own mind, though. In past years he had grown partial to it. Much of his time he had spent in solitude, wandering the weathered wilds. Everything was soon to change, however. Soon he would be lord of these lands and his kind would look to him for guidance. They would honour him.

He made to exit the hall. As he walked, the statue of Akimr crumbled to the floor behind him, obliterated by the mere desire for it in his mind. It was soon to be replaced with a statue of his own figure; of one worthy to stand above all others.

9

THE LONELY PROVINCE

The morning was cold. Mist submerged the valley. The nearby vegetation was still and white; covered in fine crystals of frozen dew. At this elevation winter was already tightening its grip over the tender land.

When Aldrick had woken, Télia was absent and her bed left neat. He had found her in the stable, accompanied by Sinin and Aru. The three of them were readying their horses in silence.

"Good morning," he said, greeting none of them in particular.

"Hello, Al," said Sinin dully. "Promise me something, will you? Never drink as much as I did last night." He groaned and rubbed his forehead. "I feel like there is an axe lodged in my skull."

Aldrick laughed. "Very well—I promise, but only because I don't think I could if I tried."

Télia shot Sinin a disapproving glance. "You're a

drunk, you know that don't you? You need help."

Sinin frowned. "I am not a drunk. A drunk is someone who is always drunk. I am a drank. I drank last night and am paying the price today."

"Well it's a fair price. Don't whine about it."

"Did you say wine?"

Télia shook her head and tried not to grin. "You're a lost cause."

Aldrick found himself downcast by the way the two spoke to each other—as though they were overly familiar with one another. He wondered how close they had been in the past. Realising it was a foolish and immature thing to dwell on he tried to push it from his mind.

"Aldrick, are you ready to ride?" Aru asked, ignoring them as they continued to squabble.

"Not so much, no. I'll head back inside and get my things."

"Yes, do that."

When he re-entered the house Jon was walking down the stairs clutching a sizable assortment of things in his arms. He wore his grand wielding robes once more.

"Good morning Aldrick," he said brightly. "I hope it has greeted you well."

"And you," Aldrick replied. "Can I help you carry any of that?"

"No, no, I am quite fine, thank you. Just let me put this down. I have something for you." Jon rested his load by the door then took a small book from the top of the pile and handed it to Aldrick. "Here. This belongs to you. I have kept it for many years. It was your father's arcane journal, something scholars of Delthendra are given to write an account of their experiences with the world of wielding. I found it within the ruins of this place. Your mother must have kept it with her after he passed."

Aldrick took the journal in surprise and wonder. It was leather bound. On the cover was a faded symbol that appeared as a globe with a number of curving lines originating from the centre and weaving around the edge, like crawling vines. Beneath this were his father's initials, G A, inscribed in a bold font. He carefully opened the journal to a random page. It was singed at the edges and much of it had been browned and cracked by heat. In one place an entry of messy writing scribed with a fine quill was discernible, though exactly what it read was not.

"Thank you for this, Jon," Aldrick said, closing the journal equally as carefully.

Jon smiled. "Not a problem, my boy. I had completely forgotten about it until now. I thought it might offer you some insight into your father's life, and perhaps also some valuable teachings, that is, if you are able to read any of it."

"Hopefully. I will look through it when I can. I ought to pack now. I won't be long."

"Very good. I'll meet you by the stable. Take all the time you need and remember to close the door behind you. The others have no need to return." Jon picked up his things and exited.

Aldrick took very little time. Much of his gear had

been untouched since the journey here. After fetching some fruit and bread he found left in the kitchen, he carried everything, including the weighty longsword Télia had bought him in Farguard, out to the stable. The others had already mounted their horses and trotted about in the frosty grass nearby.

When Aldrick's gear was all loaded on, he patted his loyal steed on the neck.

"Looks like we're off again, chum," he said. Tame neighed heartily and flicked his head excitedly. Aldrick mounted and joined the others.

"Are you ready?" asked Télia, bringing De'ama to a standstill at his side.

He took a breath. "Yes."

"Well then, let us be off!" Jon prompted his chestnut mare forward with a firm pat on the neck and their quest was commenced.

Aldrick's heart pounded. This was it. It had been but a small step leaving his home and coming this far. Now, they were truly venturing into the unknown. There would be no more safe havens to stop at. No more familiar faces to greet along the way. He wished to see his family one last time and say goodbye, but it was far too late for that. Perhaps if they came upon a village he could send them a letter by wing—tell them why he was doing this, tell them not to worry and bid them farewell in the most fitting way he was able with a quill. If not, he could only hope that there would be a return journey.

Jon led them through the clearing, whereupon they met the mountain path and followed it northward. The land soon began to slope gently and the trees closed in around them. Though the mist thinned beneath their branches, the way darkened. Until it fully lifted from the valley basin the morning light would not reach them.

While they traversed the cold and the shade, Aldrick found comfort in knowing Télia was near. There were moments when he was certain he smelt the faint summery aroma of her hair upon the still air. It soothed his nerves.

Hours had passed before the mist finally subsided. The forest lightened and dazzling rays of sunlight began to flood the ground, transforming dewdrops into rising spirals of steamy vapour which lingered only momentarily before dispersing. Above them, the canopy had become alive with the chatter of birds. A few, including a black fantail that looked identical to the one that had shown Aldrick the path to his mother's grave, followed them, flitting happily between the lower branches. At times the birds would dart across the path in front of them and chirp loudly, as if to boast of their courage.

Shortly after noon the company came upon a steep bank, down which the path wound two and fro to meet a stream. Aldrick could see over the tops of the trees and on down the valley. It continued a fair distance before the mountains gradually arced eastward.

"We shan't be going that way," Jon said. "It leads you too far from your destination. Though I wish to reach Galdrem as soon as I can, I will accompany you to Blackbed first. We leave the mountains here." He turned his horse left to follow a muddy track Aldrick had failed to notice.

"Where does this lead?" asked Sinin.

"It is a shortcut that will take us into the Lonely Province," Jon replied over his shoulder, "an old hunter's passage which leads between the peaks."

Soon enough they were deep within a narrow ravine which had, over the ages, been carved through earth and stone between the mountains. Its walls were covered in green moss, except for along their bases where floodwater passed frequently enough to prevent anything living from claiming a permanent hold. Here, veins of a dull golden mineral could be seen running through stone. Aldrick put out his hand and picked at some, only to find it was surprisingly flaky and turned into a fine paste when pressed.

"No, it's not gold, sadly," Jon informed Télia, who was also examining it keenly. "It is called mica—very common in the highlands."

Télia looked rather disappointed and continued on. Aldrick smiled to himself, watching her ride away. She was... inexpressibly faultless. Her emotions shone from her with ease, yet there was rarely a moment when he could tell exactly what she was thinking. Perhaps this was one reason she lingered in his mind so often.

In time the walls of the ravine receded and they found themselves surrounded by foliage once more. The sun had followed them to this side of the mountains and eyed them through the branches ahead. Fortunately, the track wound down the slope in a northward direction and they were spared from its glare.

When they emerged from the trees, a breathtaking view greeted them. Aldrick had envisioned the Lonely Province as a dull and solemn place. However, it was quite the contrary. Gentle hills, painted in vibrant green long grass rolled far into the distance. Between these hills, shady meadows flourished and streams trickled, searching for lower lands. In the north, a great river meandered toward the western coast—a silver grass snake in the afternoon sun.

Télia gasped. "Beautiful."

Jon also gazed on in marvel. "Isn't it? A place of serenity, though that is an illusion severed by a knowledge of its past. Great battles were waged in these lands. We may very well find ourselves treading upon some of the battlefields."

"This was during the civil wars?" Aldrick asked.

Jon nodded. "Yes. They were the bloodiest times in our history."

"So far," said Aru, speaking for the first time since morning. "Let us not forget why we are here."

"I'm quite sure none of us have," Sinin said dismissively. "There is no reason not to enjoy this journey while we're on it. I just wish we had thought to bring the rest of the wine along with us."

Télia hit him hard on the shoulder.

"Ouch," he said in barefaced sarcasm.

Jon dismounted and stretched his back. "Well, we may have no wine but we do have food and water. Come—let us refresh ourselves before continuing. We will ride with haste for the remainder of the afternoon."

They spoke little as they rested. As well as the beautiful view, thoughts of the road ahead kept their minds occupied. Aldrick was thinking on Jon's forthcoming departure and wishing it didn't have to be so. He knew the Blackbed Plains weren't far away. The distant north-western horizon was draped in a murky haze—a foreshadowing of the dark terrain below. Did they stand a chance in such a place without Jon's wisdom and wizardry? Only time would tell.

A strong breeze, heard first as a wave of rustling branches travelling down the mountainside, swept past them and transformed the fields beyond into a rippling ocean of green.

"We had best continue on," said Jon after admiring the display for a while.

They stood and summoned their horses. Télia, Sinin and Aru whistled to theirs in a way Aldrick had never heard. It was high pitched, though achieved without using one's fingers. Their horses quickly responded, bolting back at a gallop. De'ama seemed particularly driven and won their imaginary race. When she reached Télia, the mare pranced around in circles, singing her own praises.

"The wind excites her," said Télia, patting her softly on the neck. "It gives her wings."

Without warning Sinin had a sword drawn and was facing the forest behind them.

Jon strode to him. "What is it, Sinin?"

"We have a follower."

As swiftly as Sinin had drawn his sword, Télia and Aru had crossbows in hand. Télia grabbed Aldrick's arm and pulled him sideways to the cover of a solitary boulder. Turning back, he saw Jon seize his staff and drop down into the grass by his horse. Aldrick drew a knife from his belt and rested his back against the boulder. Télia crouched and readied her crossbow beside him.

"We're in a bad position here," she said, distressed. "Our visitor has the forest as cover."

Aldrick listened for the sound of movement within the trees but the rush of the wind through their leaves drowned out all else—another disadvantage. With any hope, whoever approached was not yet aware they had been compromised.

Looking sideways, Aldrick saw Sinin and Aru stooped in the grass alongside Jon, using the slant of the hill as cover. They were motionless, attention fixed upon the treeline. He lifted his head slightly and peered in the same direction.

After a nervous wait, a figure on horseback emerged from the trees. No sooner had it done so than Jon was on his feet, his staff raised in hand. There was a cry and the figure lifted from the horse and dangled upside down in mid-air with arms and cloak reaching for the ground.

Suddenly Aldrick realised who it was.

"Jon, put him down!" he shouted urgently, jumping out from cover. "That's Kaal, you fool!"

Jon stared at him in shock. "What?"

"It's my brother! Put him down!"

Jon's staff fell and so did Kaal, rather violently, to the ground.

Aldrick sprinted to him. "Kaal, bloody hell, Kaal, what are you doing here?" He heaved his brother to his feet and brushed him off.

"What... there... just... happened to me...?" Kaal stammered. "Aldrick, is that you?" He pushed back his mess of black hair and stared at Aldrick in total bewilderment.

Aldrick grinned. "Yes, it sure is. How in all hell did you find us here?"

Kaal wiped his pale face and sat himself back on the ground. "I tracked horses... Aldrick, what happened just then? Didn't you see? I was lifted into the air."

Now Aldrick tried not to grin. "That was some of Jon's magical powers. Sorry, he didn't recognise you."

Kaal's face was void of expression. "Magical powers," he repeated.

"Yes. He is a wizard, remember? I mean wielder."

Kaal didn't respond. He looked beyond Aldrick to where Jon stood in the grass, dressed in his robes, holding his staff.

Aldrick took the reins of Kaal's horse and started walking back to the others. "Come on, I'll introduce you to everyone."

They congregated where they had first sat to rest. Kaal kept at Aldrick's side, visibly uneasy.

Jon came and embraced him. "Kaal, it has been too long. Sorry for lifting you off your steed just now. I wasn't expecting it to be you. What a pleasant surprise this is."

"You... you are truly a wielder, Jon?" Kaal asked him in awe.

Jon grinned. "Yes indeed... surprise!"

Aldrick took a breath. Now was as good a time as any. "I am too, as it turns out..."

Kaal stared at him.

"Oh, really? That's good," he said vaguely. He was in deep shock now. His pupils were wider than Aldrick had even seen them.

"I suppose it is." Aldrick gestured to the others. "These are aeras, hired to protect me—Sinin, Aru and Télia. Télia you already know, of course."

Kaal nodded at them but avoided eye contact.

"This is your brother, Aldrick?" Sinin stepped forward and opened his arms to Kaal. Kaal didn't move.

"He is."

"Obviously not a blood brother, right?" asked Aru obnoxiously. "Otherwise you wouldn't be so special."

"No he isn't." Aldrick thumped Kaal on the back. "But we are brothers all the same."

"Why is he here?"

"No, why are you here?" asked Kaal, regaining control of his words. He glanced round at them all. "I was expecting to find Aldrick at Jon's house."

Aldrick was unsure of how best to respond.

"We are kind of... on a quest," he said, almost as a question.

"To rid the world of an evil wielder," added Télia.

"I should have guessed," Kaal said, flinging his hands in the air.

"I know how you're feeling, Brother," Aldrick reassured him.

Aru leant in close to Jon. "We don't have time for this, and we certainly haven't space for another in our company. There is little he can offer us."

Kaal had overhead her.

"I am here for my brother," he said firmly. "I'm sticking with him wherever he goes." He turned to Aldrick. "Father sent me to watch over you after he returned. He failed to mention any quests, though."

"Well, there have been some recent developments."

"You didn't think to come home before gallivanting off across the Narathlands?"

"I did, but we are pressed for time, very pressed."

Kaal glared at him with a firmly locked jaw for a time, then sighed and crossed his arms. "So what's going on? Tell me more about this 'evil wielder' your mystery woman mentioned."

After convincing the others there was time to spare, Aldrick tried his best to enlighten Kaal to the whole story so far, emphasising his sole ability to drain Malath's storm in an attempt to justify his partaking in the quest. The whole time Kaal listened in silence, as he himself had when Jon told him much of this.

When Aldrick finished speaking Kaal simply said "Uh ha," before continuing with "So, I guess finding this half stone thing is a reasonable move, considering Malath sounds like some kind of maddened god. But in all honesty, it sounds as though we are done for either way, going on what you've said."

"I'm liking this positivity."

Kaal managed a grin. "Do you feel like you're up to the task? Will you actually be able to absorb Malath's... storm power stuff?"

He shrugged. "We're all hoping so."

Jon came to them. "It is time to go, lads."

Aldrick looked to the others, who were waiting on horseback. Aru looked very impatient. Télia appeared the contrary. Her eyes were closed and she was singing a soft song to herself. Her hair was caught in the breeze and danced gracefully around her face. He couldn't make out any of the lyrics to the song, but the melody was beautiful and somewhat haunting. It almost sounded like a lament.

When he and Kaal had mounted their horses, the six of them set off down the lower mountainside. At its base they picked up their pace and began a swift journey across the undulating fields of the Lonely Province. The wind was now at their backs, spurring them forward. Jon led but De'ama frequently galloped ahead, whinnying stubbornly in response to Télia's efforts to slow her. She was a free spirit.

Shortly before sunset, Aldrick noticed some strange objects bridging the horizon ahead of them. Haphazardly spaced between two broad hills, they rose from the ground; some wide, some thin, all the light tones of marble. It soon became apparent that these were the ruins of some ancient city, the nearest of which being one half of a great archway. Upon reaching this, the six companions slowed to a trot and proceeded into the ruins.

Covering the ground was a plethora of blooms of

colours ranging from the deepest of reds to faint blues and tepid yellows. Some species Aldrick recognised from gardens in Rain, but others were unknown to him. There was also an abundance of leafy fruit trees, all of which displayed an impressive crop of well-ripened pome fruits. Many served as host to vines which twisted their stems firmly around the tree's trunks and dangled their fragrant bouquets of blossoms at head height. Jon picked a selection of these as they wandered by and presented them to Aru.

"Thanks," she said stiffly.

"Was this Prithe?" Aldrick asked, trying to distract Jon from the awkwardness that followed.

"Oh no," Jon replied, seemingly unfazed by Aru's reaction. "No, Prithe's ruins lie to the northeast. This was Alimare, The Fruitful City."

"Named so because of all the fruit?" asked Sinin, before taking a hearty bite out of a pear he had just picked.

"Because of cultivation in general. Here the soil is deep and healthful. Old books account this city as the storage place for all winter food supplies for every city and township west of the ranges. Many of the ruins you see around you were likely the great storehouses which sheltered it. Unfortunately, they offered no shelter from an army that sacked the city months before taking Prithe, which by then was suffering from malnutrition and disease."

"I have never quite understood why this land remains deserted, even after so long," said Télia. "It offers wealth and wonder."

"Well, there are two reasons," started Jon. "Firstly, the majority of settlements which grew after the demise of Prithe did so close to the coastline. And secondly, people believed this province to be cursed after the cities fell. They believed that evil had seeped into the soil from Blackbed and fated it to be so."

Aru snorted.

"Foolish thinking," she remarked. "Nothing but groundless superstition."

"*Ground* superstition," corrected Sinin, winking.

There was a silence.

They were soon in the heart of the ruins. A small stream wandered across their path, shallow enough for the horses to cross with ease. Along its edges, clumps of lush grass grew and the nearby trees stood tall, offering shelter from the breeze. Strangely, there were few birds to be heard singing.

"We will camp here tonight," Jon said, coming to a halt and looking around.

They dismounted, unsaddled their horses and left them to roam free. Aldrick realised he had brought only a pillow and no blanket but decided that his cloak, along with the bulky grass would keep him comfortable when he rested. Both he and Kaal were well accustomed to spending a clear night under the stars. They had often done so as children, waiting patiently for falling stars and pondering the nature of Solemn, The Pale Moon.

"Ahh, camping is the very best thing." Télia dropped her things and spun around with her arms outstretched. "We should have a fire tonight!"

"Yes," agreed Jon. "A light to honour the peoples who once made this city a marvel."

"We still don't have any wine," grumbled Sinin, unenthusiastically opening his flask of water.

After he had also refreshed himself, Aldrick turned his attention to Kaal, who had neither spoken nor smiled since they left the ranges.

"Are you all right, Brother?" he asked, walking to his side.

Kaal was somewhere far off in the distance.

"Everything is changing, isn't it?" he asked after a time. "The world has found us, and it's bigger than we ever imagined."

Aldrick sighed. "It is."

"And whoever thought that you'd be its saviour."

"I wish it wasn't so."

"And what else do you wish was never so?" Kaal asked, now turning to meet Aldrick's eye. "Should Braem and Phelvara never have raised you? Should we not have been brothers? Should you have lived the privileged life of a wielder in the north?!"

Aldrick was taken aback by Kaal's words, but only momentarily. He understood that, like himself, Kaal was finding recent revelations difficult to come to terms with. He didn't wish to give his brother the impression that he was actually enjoying any of this, which, truthfully, he wasn't... except perhaps for being in Télia's company.

"I was content with life before the ka-zchen attack, you know that. I am here now because I can help, and because I wish to avenge my birth parents. Somehow...

I miss them. But that doesn't mean I resent having the family I do now."

Kaal didn't reply. He looked at the ground with an expression of indifference until Aldrick walked away, annoyed. He went and stood by Jon, where he sat beneath an old apple tree.

"Hello, my boy," Jon said warmly. "How are we?"

Aldrick shrugged.

"I'm fine," he fumed, then, feeling motivated, "I have to learn more, Jon—my mother's ability."

"Indeed." Jon heaved himself to his feet. He plucked an apple from a branch above him and ignited it with storm. "Go on—take my storm and starve the flame," he challenged.

Aldrick watched the fiery fruit for a moment then cocked his head from left to right, preparing himself. He knew he could take Jon's storm and he was going to take Jon's storm. He pointed both palms directly at Jon's chest and willed it from him... nothing happened. The apple continued to burn a bright yellow and spit boiling juice.

"You can do it, Aldrick," encouraged Télia.

He tried again, concentrating without falter. The apple went on burning. Suddenly part of it popped and sizzling skin flew into his face. He let out a cry of pain and wiped it from him. The apple fell to the ground, smouldering.

He stared up at Jon. "Did you do that?"

Jon was smiling down at him. He shook his head. "No my boy, you did."

Télia and Sinin clapped and cheered.

"You're almighty now, Al," Sinin said in jest.

Aldrick felt woozy. Such a fleeting success had drained much of his energy. He sat. "I'm hun—" His words were cut off as a fresh apple fell on his head. "Thanks, Jon."

While he ate, Aldrick reflected on the achievement. They had been correct yesterday when speculating that a purpose was needed in order for him to wield the ability. He needed to feel threatened and self-protective, just as his mother had. Perhaps this would prove easier in the presence of Malath, who would likely be bent on crushing him or turning him into a human torch on sight.

Télia walked up to him carrying two swords, one of which was his. "So your wielding is coming along nicely, but how handy are you with a blade? I will teach you now." She spoke in an assertive voice that made him briskly leap to his feet and take his sword. Its blade almost met the ground when she unhanded it.

She focused on teaching him basic defence. First, rather embarrassingly, she showed him how to grip the hilt correctly, and then a number of blade motions and allied body stances which she promised could deflect the most basic of attacks. All of these moves had peculiar names which he failed to remember, so Télia resorted to yelling them out as numbers when she came at him so he could react accordingly. It was obvious to him that she was talented with a blade. Her attacks were swift and fluent. This prompted him to focus on quickening his own pace.

They were able to continue into the dusk as Sinin

and Aru, with a little help from Jon, had built an impressive fire that spilt warmth and light across the campsite.

While Aldrick knelt during a brief break Télia had reluctantly permitted, Jon came and stooped beside him so their heads were near. "You know, wielding storm and wielding weapons don't necessarily have to be separate practises, my boy." He said it not as a whisper, but quietly enough that Télia did not hear.

"What do you mean?" Aldrick asked.

Jon patted him on the shoulder. "Think on it."

"Time to go again." Télia thrust Aldrick's sword back into his weary hands.

Standing again, he felt a sudden burst of determination. This time had to be different. He needed advantage over Télia's skill. What exactly had Jon mean? Wield his storm while he fought? Yes, he would give that a try.

"I know exactly what I'm doing," he told himself. He gripped his sword firmly and took stance, planning to fuel the blade's motion with gravity.

"One!" Télia lunged at him.

Aldrick swung his blade at hers. There was an air-splitting clang before it flew from her hands and disappeared into the darkness above. She let out a startled cry and shook her hands.

"Cheater!" she yelled, half in anger, half in humour.

He dropped his sword, grabbed her hands and frantically began caressing them. "I'm sorry!"

Jon stood and raised one hand to the skies. "I think you have forgotten something, Aldrick."

They heard the spinning sound of Télia's airborne blade before it hurtled back into view, stopping a short distance above Jon's hand.

"Whoops," said Aldrick.

"That was most impressive!" Jon returned the sword to Télia. "That is how you fight—by using what advantages you have! Maybe next time also try igniting the blade."

"No, do that when you fight an actual enemy," said Télia. "I'm all done, at least for now, anyway."

"Truly, I am sorry," restated Aldrick, feeling terribly guilty.

She knocked him lightly on the shoulder. "Don't worry, I'll have my revenge."

They joined Sinin, Kaal and Aru by the fire, all of whom had been avid spectators.

"Violence is not the answer, you two," Kaal remarked. He was grinning. What was bothering him earlier seemed to have passed. Aldrick sat down beside him.

While the fire's embers drifted peacefully into the night sky, the six of them sat in a half-circle around its flickering heart, talking cheerfully, laughing; avoiding talk of the journey ahead of them. Inevitably it would resume at the break of dawn. Until then, all was well.

Unlike the previous night they slept early, worn out from the lengthy day of travel. Sinin agreed to stay on guard as a precaution and Kaal begrudgingly agreed to take his place in the early hours of the morning after losing a game of stone, blade and parchment to Télia. She was delighted with her win and skipped off happily to arrange a place to sleep. To Aldrick's delight, this proved to be right beside him.

"You don't mind if I stay close, do you?" she asked as she lay down. We've slept on the same bed before so it shouldn't bother you too much... it's so I can protect you," she quickly added.

"It doesn't bother me," he said calmly.

After a short time in which only the cracking of heated wood and Jon's snoring was to be heard, Télia turned on her side so her waterfalls of ebony hair faced him.

"Goodnight," she whispered, already half taken by sleep. "Be at peace in your dreams."

"And you. Goodnight."

10

PIRATES

Someone was yelling. Aldrick leapt up in alarm. The others were rummaging around the campsite. It was so early stars still lingered in the pallid sky.

"Curse them!" Sinin kicked the charred remains of a log from the fire bed.

Télia was looking beyond the campsite. "Where is Kaal?"

Aru snorted. "Supposedly still on guard duty. Jolly good job he did."

"What's going on?" Aldrick asked.

"We've been robbed."

"Robbed?" He looked around. "What's been taken?"

"My staff," Jon said angrily.

"Only that?"

"Yes, it is all anyone would need to make a fair sum of money."

"We are fortunate that whoever took it was not an assassin," Aru said heatedly. "Otherwise we would all have woken in the Life Afterwards!"

At that moment Kaal came bolting into view, his bow in hand.

"What's... happened? What's going on?" he asked between heavy breaths.

Aru stormed up to him. "We have been robbed, that is what. Jon's staff is missing and it is all thanks to you and your lack of observation skills. What have you been doing? Having a wee snooze?"

Kaal looked awkward. "I didn't think there was anyone nearby. I've been on the hillside keeping watch over the entire ruins."

"But not over us," Aru snapped.

"Calm down, Aru," Télia demanded, walking to them. "Obviously someone with some skill in thievery has taken Jon's staff. We couldn't expect Kaal to have been prepared for that, especially out here in this deserted land."

Aru glared at Kaal. "Be thankful that the culprit did not decide you were an obstacle in their way."

Sinin had been examining the ground a short way downstream.

"Kaal, did you walk here last night?" he asked.

Kaal shook his head.

Jon went to Sinin. "What is it?"

Sinin pointed to the edge of the stream. "They followed the streambed up to reach our camp. This is where they got out and back in."

"Clever—treading water to conceal their path."

Sinin nodded. "They might even be a professional."

Jon shook his head. "No, a professional is hired by somebody and I doubt anybody with the money to do so has knowledge of my staff, nor of my location. This was an opportune theft—the work of a relic hunter or perhaps a lone marauder."

"A thief all the same," said Télia.

"We should track them down and end them," Sinin proposed.

Jon strode back to the campsite. "Yes, we must find them at once. Without that staff I will have little defence against our foes in Galdrem." He hurriedly began packing his gear.

Aldrick and the others followed suit. In short time they were on horseback, setting off downstream. Sinin led, followed by Jon, both of whom hung low to one side of their horse, scouting for further tracks left by the thief. There were none to be found.

"What if they were clever about this and came from the other direction?" suggested Télia.

Sinin clicked his finger and pointed at her. "Good point."

"We must split up," said Jon.

Aru sighed. "There is no time for this," she muttered.

Jon ignored her. "Sinin, Télia, Aldrick, you go upstream. Kaal, Aru, we will continue down. Keep your eyes peeled, all of you."

They parted ways. Aldrick and Télia followed Sinin steadily upstream, back past the campsite toward the western outskirts of the ruins. It wasn't long before they had left the last stray stone behind them and found themselves at the foot of one of the inclosing hills. Here, the stream trickled from a small pond that hid beneath lily pads.

"Look!" Télia pointed to a clump of grass at the edge of the pond. It showed clear signs of disturbance. "The thief was here."

"No," said Sinin. "More than one." He pointed further on to where the grass had been heavily trodden. "There was a company on horseback." He turned and whistled the same shrill whistle Aldrick had heard the aeras use yesterday when summoning their horses. A few moments later the others appeared, galloping toward them.

"They came this way. There were many," informed Sinin.

Jon tugged on his reins and his mare reared. "Well, let's pursue!" He assumed the lead.

Their pace was hurried. The sun was rising and rays of golden light spilt over the Midland Ranges, flooding their path as they wove between the hills.

Suddenly, and very unexpectedly, Jon halted. His mare neighed and reared back once more. The others abruptly followed suit. Aldrick looked ahead to see what had compelled Jon to stop. His eyes fell upon a group of mounted travellers. There were about twenty of them heading their way. They did not travel lightly. With them were a number of horses which carried only gear.

About fifty paces ahead of them, the travellers halted and silence ensued. Each company surveyed the other.

"Watch for concealed movements. There is no doubt they carry weapons," said Sinin in a half whisper, one hand falling to his side.

"And there is little doubt one of those is my staff," added Jon.

"They aren't able to use it though, right?" asked Kaal.

"Thankfully not."

"Let us offer them a simple deal," began Sinin. "They part with the staff, or, we part their heads from their bodies."

Télia shot him a glance. "How very poetic."

There was no need to press the riders to confess their culpability. One of them, a portly man, slipped off his horse and held up Jon's staff in one hand, flaunting his possession of it.

"Have ya come lookin' for this?!" he yelled out to them. "It's a mighty fine piece. I oughta tell you off for not keepin' it under more watchful eyes." His slovenly accent was one Aldrick had never heard before.

Jon trotted forward a short way.

"You are quite correct—we are looking for that," he said as civilly as was able in a raised voice. "We would have had more watchful eyes upon it, only we thought we were far from the hands of any thieves."

"Thieves?!" the man exclaimed. "Oh no, we ain't no thieves. In fact, we think you are. We saw ya layin' in our home, takin' th' benefits of our trees 'nd their wood. We just thought we'd take somethin' back is all." He turned to his companions. "Ain't that right, fellas? We're just keepin' some kinda order out 'ere."

There were some 'Ayes' of agreement.

Jon crossed his hands. "So you think Alimare is your home, do you?"

"Yes, 'nd rightfully so," the man said bluntly. "We b'n comin' 'ere for th' cold months since years I c'n 'ardly remember. There be plenty of underground shelter 'nd we are the few who know how ta find it."

"I see. And where do you call home when you are away from here?"

The man laughed. "Well th' ocean, course!"

Télia stirred. "Pirates."

Sinin snorted. "What a lousy bunch."

Jon turned back to them, uncrossing his hands. "Have your weapons ready, friends. This will likely get messy."

The pirate begged their attention once more. "Now, I hope you ain't thinkin' of doin' nothin' rash." He stowed the staff away on his horse. "We been only kind to ya thus far. We were hopin' to avoid trouble."

Télia trotted forward. "You were hoping to avoid trouble? You've stolen something from us! How is that avoiding trouble?!" There were deathly notes in her voice.

The pirate chuckled. "Like we said, lass, we were just intendin' on maintainin' some kinda order. You take from us, we take from you."

"But the ruins aren't yours!" she cried. "They belong to nobody!"

"Nothin' is nobodies, lass." He mounted his horse. "Now, you 'nd ya friends oughta hurry along before we change our minds 'bout bein' friendly 'bout all this." His tone was more sinister now.

"I'm afraid we won't be hurrying along," said Jon firmly. "The staff shall be returned to me now."

The pirate glanced round at his crew. "Oh, will it? Well come 'nd get it, then. But I 'ope you realise you be well outnumbered, 'nd you ain't got no good power in ya without ya staff in ya hand, so just what ya gonna do? Come any closer and we'll end all of ya!"

The pirates raised armed bows. Immediately, the aera's crossbows were in hand, aiming straight back at them. Aldrick and Kaal hurried to ready their own.

"Now might be a good time to wish we had shields," Sinin muttered grimly.

Jon raised a hand, signalling for them to hold.

The pirate sniggered. "Ya not seriously considerin' fightin', are ya? What can one single magic maker 'nd 'is band of misfits do 'gainst us 'nd all our arrows?"

"We'll see," Jon said quietly. Without turning his head he addressed Aldrick. "Aldrick, my boy, if you see him signal to fire, help me create a warding wall in front of us."

Aldrick was confused. "A warding wall?"

"Yes, as I have taught you, by manipulating gravity. Help me shield us from their arrows."

"I'll try."

"Try hard," muttered Sinin.

"Just remember your training," Jon said calmly. He remained composed.

Aldrick was anything but. This was some serious responsibility he had been given.

Télia glanced at Jon. "Perhaps we should retreat. This is dangerous and unnecessary."

Jon shook his head. "They will not have the staff."

Télia grumbled. Aldrick approved of her bid for a passive resolution.

The pirate rested his arms across the neck of his horse.

"Ya know—" He paused to yawn. "I've suddenly found m'self growin' tired of you lot. I'm thinkin' we oughta just clear ya out of our path 'nd see what else valuable 'nd usable ya have on ya. If that young lass happens to survive, 'nd even if she don't for that matt'r, I'll put her to some fine use."

Aldrick could make out a smirk ripe across the pirate's filthy face. He was enraged. It was almost worse than that night at Jon's—overpowering. He would end the loathsome brute! No one the likes of him would come within an arm's reach of Télia! In a flash Aldrick drew his arrow and without a thought it became fire. He released it for the pirate. With fatal speed it struck his chest and sent him somersaulting backwards into his crew. For a moment they were in shock, and then they retaliated. A flurry of arrows were returned. Aldrick waved his hand and they were deflected into the grass.

"Fire!" yelled Jon.

Arrows now flew from Kaal's and the aera's bows. A number of the pirates fell from their horses. More arrows came at them. Aldrick deflected them again. More pirates fell. A remaining few turned and fled. Victory was theirs!

Jon trotted to where the pirate captain's horse reared wildly amid the fallen bodies. He came alongside it and retrieved his staff from a saddle bag. Aldrick and the others approached.

Looking down at the bodies, Aldrick felt strangely hollow. He didn't feel for any of these men. They had all gotten what was coming to them, especially the captain. They were worthless pirates. Their lives held little importance to him. They had stood in the way of more pressing concerns. He looked at his brother. Kaal appeared much more distraught. His face was white. His bow was still clenched in his fist. Aldrick realised that this was the first time Kaal had witnessed death, let alone shared in the dealing of it. Seeing him this way made Aldrick guilty of his own seemingly untroubled conscience. Maybe it was nerves that had stolen his emotion, for now a sickening feeling began to seep through him. These people lay dead! They were gone from this world, never to return. Had they all embodied black souls, or had they simply sought to avenge their leader?

Sinin had been examining the bodies. He stood and sighed. "Well, looks like that's the end of them."

"Not quite." Aru was standing over one that lay a little way from the rest. She stooped and ran a blade into the man's chest. There was a stifled grunt and then silence.

For a while no one spoke. Aldrick trotted back a short distance to where Télia sat on her mare, staring away across the hills. Kaal followed.

She looked across at him. Her face was tender.

"There are times when I see death as the end of hope," she said solemnly. A tear fell from one of her eyes. "It is always so unnecessary." She turned her face away.

Aldrick understood now that she had been equally as affected by the deaths of the men in the coastal inn, but had hidden it in an attempt to comfort him. This time it was too much. Suddenly he felt more deeply for her than ever before. He wanted to console her — see her tears gone and her heart warmed. He had no idea how to achieve this so he simply rested a hand on her shoulder.

Kaal was silent at his side, staring out into the distance as Télia had been.

"Are you all right?" Aldrick asked.

Kaal nodded faintly.

Jon came to them.

"It is time to move on," he said. There was a tone of softness and understanding in his voice. "We should reach Old Capital Road by noon."

"That is where you leave us," Aldrick said cheerlessly.

"Yes. I must reach Galdrem and assist the Synod."

Télia turned and faced Jon head on.

"Jon, why?" she asked forcefully. "Why was the staff so important?"

Jon looked down.

"I…" he began. "I need it."

"So you would risk all of our lives for it?"

"No." Jon looked up at her earnestly. "No, there was little risk. I offered Aldrick the opportunity to further realise his wielding abilities. Without his competence, all of us are doomed. There is little doubt of that."

Télia glared at him then rode away.

Aldrick repeated Jon's words in his head.

"You wanted me to further realise my abilities?" he asked.

Jon nodded. "I did not foresee your temper besting you the way it did, but yes, I wanted you to practise wielding under pressure and danger. You were outstanding."

Aldrick didn't feel like he had done anything outstanding. In fact, wielding had been fairly effortless in those moments. Perhaps that was exactly what Jon had wanted. It could only be a good thing—wielding was beginning to feel more natural. He was more in touch with his storm, more confident in himself. Taking life was not something he wanted to ever feel natural, though. He hoped never to have to do it again, but knew well that he would. It was why he was here.

11

BLACKBED

The grass was no longer green. Instead, it was pale yellow and dry. In many places none grew at all and the surface of the earth was left dry and cracked. The borders of Old Capital Road were difficult to distinguish. Only the faint and infrequent marks of carriage wheels hinted at its path. Clearly the road had received little traffic in recent years. Aldrick supposed this was because few were comfortable treading so close to the Blackbed Plains. He could sense them looming just beyond a ridgeline to the northeast. Over the ridge, an eerie silence seeped that boded evil.

"Your path lies that way," told Jon, pointing in that exact direction. He was sitting on his mare, facing them, soon to go his own way. It had been only hours since they encountered the thieving pirates and Aldrick wished for more time with him before continuing into more treacherous territory.

"Surely we need not all venture into Blackbed," said Aru. "Four of us following one young wielder on a doubtful expedition to find an elusive stone seems rather rash. I propose you have company on your journey to Galdrem, Jon."

Aldrick found himself agreeing with her. "Yes, I don't need all of you following me around." He looked at Jon. "You should have your own protection."

"Perhaps," Jon said tentatively.

"So who is it to be?" asked Sinin.

Aru turned to him. "You," she stated.

Sinin raised his eyebrows. "Me? Why me?"

"Télia and Kaal belong at Aldrick's side. That is clear. I have wandered through those cursed plains before. I even stepped foot into Fort Blackbed many years ago. I can offer them invaluable guidance. You are the one remaining with great skill in combat. You will prove an asset to Jon."

Sinin appeared downcast. "What of my contract? I am bound to serve as aera to Al."

"Given the circumstances I think you ought not to worry about that."

"She is right, Sinin. You should go with Jon," agreed Télia. "Return home."

Sinin heaved a sigh. "Very well." He trotted to Jon's side. "It looks as though we ride together, friend."

"So be it." Jon turned and trotted a short way, distancing himself from the others, then beckoned to Aldrick.

Aldrick went, uncertainty gripping his stomach.

Jon looked upon him warmly. "My boy, this is

where we go our separate ways. You are in good hands. I wish you the very best and hope to see you again very soon."

He found no comfort in these words. "Jon, what if I cannot find the Halfstone? What if I cannot find a way?"

Jon was silent for a moment, and then he spoke gravely. "If you cannot find the stone you must run, Aldrick. Take those you hold dear under your wing and flee from these lands. I would not have you face the wrath of Malath without the advantage the stone offers at hand. It is crucial. Your odds without it are but fleeting and infinitesimal."

"But I could still help," Aldrick insisted. "There is more to worry about than Malath. There is a dragon. Everyone able to fight must fight if there is to be any hope—"

"No!" cried Jon. "Promise me you will not venture on without the stone... promise me, Aldrick!" There was a wild fear in his eyes.

Aldrick's kneejerk reaction was frustration. Jon would not make decisions for him! Yet he knew there was little point in arguing. He sighed. "I promise."

Jon's face lightened.

"Good," he said cheerily. "Now, I must be going. Remember your training, Aldrick. Remember all you have learnt and don't hesitate to practise wielding when opportunity arises... and don't ever let your guard down."

Aldrick nodded. "Farewell, Jon."

Jon hailed Sinin and raised a parting hand to the

others. When Sinin was at his side they set off together.

"I'll see you lot soon," Sinin shouted over his shoulder.

Aldrick and the others watched the two galloping away. Their figures shimmered behind an ocean of heat waves before finally melting into the horizon.

"There is no need to linger," said Aru, turning away. "Let us be off."

With her at the lead, they began to journey up the ridge and in short time were looking upon the vast barren land of the Blackbed Plains. Aldrick recalled Jon's words 'You will know that place when you see it'. The land was empty and dark. Vast areas of the ground were covered in some kind of deep black moss, or perhaps it was brittle grass, he couldn't tell. Whatever the plant was, it shrouded the earth like mats of starless night sky. It was almost as though all light that touched it was devoured. Aru, seemingly undaunted, did not hesitate before continuing down a steady slope to its outer reaches.

"Do not be stupid and try touching this stuff," she cautioned. "It is very poisonous. You need not fear for your mounts. Their hooves are tough."

"Well this place is just lovely," remarked Kaal sarcastically. He pointed to a random area of the blackness. "I can see it now. My house will be there. My children will have a play area out the back. The cattle will graze the nearby vegetation."

Aldrick and Télia chuckled heartily.

They picked up their pace. Aru retained the lead, never looking back. For hours they rode across the deathly darkness. They came upon some raised plateau-like formations on which the plant did not grow but wove between these without pausing. It wasn't until Télia called out to Aru after sundown that they finally drew to a halt.

"We must rest the horses," she insisted.

Aru turned, her lip twisted. "Very well, but do not dismount."

Télia let out a gasp of exasperation. "We could at least stretch our legs."

"No. It is possible ka-zchen are close by. They will be drawn to Aldrick's storm. We must remain mounted and aware. We will travel for much of the night. In fact, now would be a good time to check that your weapons are at the ready."

Télia crossed her arms. "When shall we rest then?"

"If you must, ride with your eyes closed," snapped Aru. "Just pray you do not suddenly feel a ka-zchen's fangs around your chest."

Télia looked liverish but said nothing. They were idle only minutes, using the time to eat and to drink fresh water that they had taken from the River Jewel earlier in the day. Aldrick had dried meats that Sinin gave him after looting the pirate's supplies but was somewhat opposed to the idea of eating a dead man's meal.

When they made way, they travelled at a slower pace. The western horizon steadily dimmed and they were soon between two blankets of darkness. Fortunately, the clouds were thin and a near full-faced Solemn had crept over the eastern horizon. The moon's pale light was just enough for them to distinguish one another's figures. Lighting torches wasn't an option—it would surrender their position to anyone or anything within a hundred leagues.

They continued on in silence. The only sound to be heard was the steady drumming of horses' hooves upon the venomous terrain. With so little to see or hear, it almost felt as though they were drifting through nothingness—a vacant dreamscape. It was weird and disconcerting.

Judging by the position of Solemn, it was around midnight when Aru finally signalled for them to stop. They were alongside another small plateau.

"We will rest here for a while upon the rock," she said. "The fort is not far away. If we stray too close in the dark we risk alerting ka-zchen guardians. Any that are there will withdraw before dawn."

Aldrick squinted ahead of them. He could barely make out the faint silhouette of a mountain in the distance. The fort was there, somewhere. As his eyes adjusted to the distance he was certain he glimpsed a twinkling speck of light.

"Someone's there!"

"It is to be expected," Aru said nonchalantly. "Malath would not have left the fort unoccupied. This was never going to be a simple matter of walking in and out again. For all we know, there is a warding enchantment placed over it."

Aldrick recalled Jon's use of the word 'enchantment' when he had told of the Shard of Heart's Storm's holding chamber.

"How exactly do warding enchantments work?" he asked.

"Quite simply—they are warding walls, only the wielder's storm is sustained within the orb on their staff rather than by way of their tireless focus."

"Wait, so..." He stopped, sensing Aru's apathy for questions. She was not a willing teacher, as Jon was.

"I will sleep first," she said, dismounting onto the rock. "Télia, take first guard."

Télia said nothing. She tetchily pulled her crossbow from her saddlebag and took up position a short distance away.

Aldrick, Kaal and Aru were soon lying upon the flat surface of the rock. It was painfully solid, even with what bedding they had brought. Sleep was elusive. Aldrick's mind dwelled on many bizarre and disturbing things, not allowing him any peace.

After no less than two hours of discomfort, he heard Aru rise and tell Télia to get some rest. She came and quietly settled herself beside him. Another hour slowly passed. Although Télia did not stir, Aldrick knew she was not sleeping; her heart beat rapidly. She likely anticipated their arrival at the fort. He feared for her. No doubt they would soon confront powerful evil. He wanted her to be safe. It was his responsibility to protect her, as much as it was hers to protect him. He could wield. He could shield her, fight for her. He would!

In the dark he felt her warm hand meet his. She tightened her delicate fingers around it and held firmly. Cool shivers washed through his body, dissolving all thought of the trials ahead. This was where he belonged—right here with her. Butterflies fluttered beneath his chest. He swallowed as quietly as he could, then softly stroked her hand with his thumb. Immediately, he felt foolish for his thumb was trembling. It was like he was sixteen again. Come on, Aldrick. Pull yourself together.

Their hands did not part for some time. He wished that they were alone together, in another place, under lighter circumstances, but would they ever have met had it not been for the reasons they did? No, probably not. This unfinished journey was the only one in which their paths crossed.

Aru had been sitting at the edge of the rock facing the direction of the fort, listening for any disturbance in the enveloping shadows.

"It is time for us to go," she said, rising to her feet all of a sudden.

Aldrick lifted his head and saw the first hint of dawn in the east. Télia withdrew her hand and stood up. She said nothing. He noticed the shape of her crossbow in her other hand. She had been on guard the whole time.

Kaal stirred. "Hell, can we not wait 'til sunup?"

"No," said Aru firmly, refastening gear to her saddle.

The others grudgingly followed suit and they were soon on their way, steadily approaching the solitary mountain. It jutted from the plains with multiple weather-worn peaks stabbing at the sky. Roughly halfway up its sharp incline, the entrance to Fort

Blackbed was marked by a stone watchtower, crowned by a square, castle-like battlement. At its base, a crumbling wall ran a short way before ending. From there, a slender path wound, to-and-fro, down to the plains below.

When the dark slopes of the mountain almost blocked all sky from view, Aru raised a hand.

"Télia and I shall go on from here," she said stiffly. "Aldrick, you and Kaal will stay and await our return."

"What if there is a warding enchantment cast over it?" Aldrick asked.

"With any luck there won't be. If there is, well, we will just have to hope you can help us pierce it."

Aru didn't sound at all optimistic about the outcome of the latter circumstance. Clearly she held little confidence in his wielding ability. That was fair enough. After all, why would she?

Télia was eying him.

"Hopefully this won't take us long," she said. "If we gain entrance we will make the path as clear for you as we can."

Aldrick clenched Tame's reins in frustration. "Do you not remember me calling for willing companions on this journey, not bodyguards?"

"Don't whinge," Aru said curtly. "We are being sensible. Please be the same."

Télia continued to look at Aldrick. A faint smile grew on her face.

"I'll see you soon," she whispered.

"Télia!" he blurted as she turned to leave. She looked back at him calmly. "… Be safe."

She beamed. "I will, Aldrick."

While he watched them riding away, Aldrick felt useless. Télia was venturing into harm's way and he was told to remain put and do nothing!

"Looks like us two can relax for a while," Kaal said, yawning heavily.

He didn't reply. His eyes were now fixed on the watchtower, surveying for movement. If he saw anything he would not stay idle.

In short time, Télia and Aru had climbed the path and vanished behind the stone wall. No warding enchantment had yet blocked their path. The succeeding moments felt like hours. Aldrick's mind echoed with dark uncertainties. What if one of Malath's wielders had seen the aeras approaching and attacked them with all the ferocity of storm? He shifted uncomfortably.

The sun had begun to rise, bathing the barbed peaks of the mountain in ominous red light. Around him and his brother, it remained cold and dim. They waited longer. Eventually the sun's light touched them.

"That's it, I'm going after them," Aldrick said, losing patience and restraint. He started forward.

"Come back, damn it!" Kaal shouted.

Aldrick kept riding.

"Stay there if you want!" he shouted back over his shoulder.

His pace was a gallop all the way up to the base of the watchtower. There, he leapt from Tame before the horse was at a standstill. De'ama and Aru's horse were close by, waiting on their masters' return. Aldrick unsheathed his sword, took a breath and made to enter. Above the arch of the entranceway was the sinister sign of Selayna, glinting callously in the sun. Only, it wasn't a sign at all. It was a drathen butterfly in the flesh that took off in a hasty flutter as he past below. It failed to enthral him. He feared only for Télia and what fate might have befallen her inside the forthcoming lair of stone.

Save for an empty weapons rack and some indistinct etchings on the wall, the interior of the tower was completely bare. There were some faint footprints on dust-covered stairs that led to the roof, but no tell-tale signs that the fort was presently occupied. In the wall to his right was a shadowy opening. Aldrick approached it with his sword at the ready. A sturdy wooden door would once have blocked his way, but was now only dry splinters on iron hinges. He stepped across the threshold and found himself in a long, gloomy passage. A number of mounted torches lined the walls, though none of them were alight.

The sound of footsteps behind Aldrick made him spin round in a frenzy. It was just Kaal. He breathed a sigh of relief then signalled him to follow. With deadly caution, they proceeded. The stillness and silence surrounding them was more a concern than a comfort. This was a haunted abode.

Soon they emerged into a vast chamber cornered by enormous, fluted stone columns. They were on the upper level. Below, accessed by stairs from all sides, was a circular floor space. In the centre of this… Télia! She lay sprawled face down on the ground, motionless.

Aldrick sprinted for her, terror flooding his veins. He was too late!

Steps from her reach he came to an abrupt stop, though not purposefully; he couldn't go on. His sword was torn from his hand. He looked around wildly. He couldn't see the culprit but knew a wielder lurked close by. Kaal had also been relieved of his weapon. Again Aldrick tried to push forward but couldn't counter the barrier of gravity that was stopping him. He let out a cry of frustration and desperation.

"Now, now, don't squawk," a sneering voice echoed from a passage above them. A gaunt wielder draped in blue robes stepped out from the shadows. He glared down at Aldrick through hateful eyes.

Aldrick's fists compressed.

"What have you done to her?!" he bellowed.

The wielder's eyes went to Télia. "Me? No. That was your friends doing."

From out of another passage walked Aru, her face stiff as ever. She was armed with her crossbow. It was pointed at Télia.

Aldrick stared at her, confused for a brief moment, then began to shake.

"You!" he roared. "Traitor! I will tear you apart!" Thunder followed his words. In the confinements of the hall it was near deafening. Aru and the wielder seemed quite unfazed by it. They continued to look down on him with loathing.

"So, this is him, is it?" The wielder marched down the stairs and surveyed Aldrick closely. "This is Isobel's child?"

Aldrick tried to punch him but failed to meet his mark.

"Please," the wielder remarked. "You insult me." His eyes narrowed and he raised a hand.

"Kagron, wait," Aru interrupted. "We must take them to our lord."

Kagron's eyes remained fixed upon Aldrick. "Must we?" he asked, irritated. "Why not just finish them here?"

"No, he may want to meet Aldrick. His sister will appreciate the others, and the sport they will offer."

Kagron scowled. "If that is what they would desire then I shan't challenge it."

Aldrick knew he couldn't let Télia or Kaal be taken anywhere.

"Get out of here!" he shouted back at Kaal.

Kaal remained put. "I'm not leav—" He was flung sideways. He struck one of the pillars and collapsed to the floor, unconscious.

Aldrick's fury deepened.

"You two are making a grave mistake," he warned.

"How is that?" asked Kagron, drawing a steel mace from his belt.

Flickers of sharp blue lightning erupted around Aldrick's fists and forearms. In the moment it was effortless to wield. It was as though he had always known this power.

Kagron took a step back, eyebrows raised. "Aru, he is more powerful than you told."

Aru walked down and pressed the tip of her crossbow against the back of Télia's head. "Try anything and she dies."

Aldrick looked at Télia's motionless figure. "How can I be certain she is alive now?"

Aru's lip curled. "She is. Only, her pretty face isn't so pretty anymore."

Relief stowed some of his anger. She was still alive. He just had to save her somehow. It was doubtful his powers were enough to defeat both Aru and Kagron. His options were few.

He allowed the lightning to fade. "Do with me as you please, but do not harm her."

Aru's crossbow remained against Télia's head for a moment longer, before she withdrew it and aimed it at Aldrick instead.

Kagron sneered.

"Time for a nap," he said, lifting his mace.

Aldrick closed his eyes and waited for the blow.

There was a whistling sound and then a thud. He opened his eyes to see Kagron dropping the mace. The wielder winced and fell to his knees. Aru lifted her crossbow and shot an arrow into the shadows. Aldrick seized the opportunity. He thrust both hands toward her violently. Like a twig in a gale, Aru flew away. She collided with a far wall and toppled to the ground in a crumpled heap.

Aldrick looked down at Kagron. The wielder whimpered on the floor, an arrow firmly lodged in his back. Now he peered in the direction Aru had fired her crossbow. Sinin was doubled over at the top of the stairs, her arrow in his chest.

Aldrick ran to him. "Sinin!"

"Hi, Al," he replied. His voice quivered. "If… if you're feeling up to the task you're welcome to try and heal me." He grinned feebly.

Aldrick knew what to do. Without hesitation he placed one hand over the wound and, with the other, pulled the arrow from Sinin's chest. Sinin let out a cry and almost fell to the floor but Aldrick held him steady, willing his wound to be healed.

After an uncertain moment Sinin beckoned for Aldrick to stop.

"All right, enough touching," he grumbled.

Aldrick withdrew his hand to find the wound had disappeared. He felt weakened but was washed with relief. He hurried back down the stairs to Télia.

A ball of fire came hurtling up at him from the hands of Kagron. The wielder was still more a threat than he had thought! In the last second Aldrick lifted his hands and created a warding wall. The fire engulfed it with raging force but failed to break through. As it subsided he saw Télia drive a dagger into Kagron's neck and, simultaneously, another arrow from Sinin pierce his chest. Kagron's eyes emptied and his body wilted.

Télia discarded the dagger and looked up at Aldrick. He could barely see her expression. Her face was drenched in blood and badly swollen. She collapsed on her side.

"Télia!" He scrambled down to her, took her in one arm and rested his free hand over her face. She had to be better. He had to make her better!

While his storm slowly healed her, he felt himself

becoming lightheaded. His vision had blurred. Slumping sideways, he fell out of consciousness.

12

HOPE LOST AND FOUND

A stinging sensation on Aldrick's cheek woke him. He blinked and peered upward. Télia was smiling down at him, her face as impeccable as ever. Strands of her hair tickled his neck.

"Did you just... slap him?"

He turned his head to see Kaal resting against a wall nearby, watching them with a big grin.

"Yes. Yes I did," said Télia. She offered Aldrick a hand. He took it and found his feet.

"Is everyone all right?" he asked.

"Yes," said Kaal perkily, rising also. "Though me least of all. Apparently Sinin and Télia were first in line for your healing storm stuff."

"Sorry. I would have got to you if I hadn't passed out."

"Don't worry. I'm fine."

Aldrick looked around the chamber. Kagron's body lay lifeless in a pool of blood. In the far corner, Sinin was binding Aru with rope where she had landed on the floor. Apparently his storm attack had not killed her.

He went to Sinin.

"Sinin, I owe you my thanks. I think all of us do. If you had not come…"

"Don't mention it," Sinin said dismissively. "I saved your life and you saved mine. We're even." He finished binding Aru, then stood and slapped Aldrick on the shoulder. "You looked to have worn yourself out back there, Al. What you did though, it was remarkable stuff. I've never seen anything like that lightning thing you did."

Aldrick looked at his hands.

"It kind of just… happened," he said. "I think it was my father's ability."

"Jon would be most impressed."

"Sinin, why did you leave Jon?" Aldrick asked. "Why did you come back?"

Sinin scratched his beard. "Well," he started. "On the way to Galdrem Jon and I got to talking about some things. He queried me about Aru, you know, because he fancies her and all. And, well, he was very surprised to learn that she is the sister of an aera he once knew—the one tasked with protecting your mother when she moved into the ranges. He believes it may have been that aera who informed Malath of her whereabouts and grew wary that Aru might also be disloyal. He sent me back to keep an eye on her. As you can see, his suspicions were correct." Sinin nodded toward Aru. "The bitch is a traitor."

Aldrick looked down at her. "I hope I didn't deal her too much harm. We may need information from her."

Sinin snorted. "I won't shed tears if she doesn't wake."

Télia and Kaal came to them.

"Yes, we will need her to talk," said Télia. She looked downcast. "Aldrick, the storm the Halfstone held could be sensed by we aeras, just as we can sense a wielder's storm." She looked around. "There is no storm in this place other than your own."

"Because the stone is probably empty... Malath has his storm back, right?"

Télia bit her lip. "Aldrick, your father's storm was in that stone too."

Aldrick's heart sunk. "Oh... I... so it's not here."

"No."

"We have looked, Al," Sinin said. "There is nothing in this place but dust and death."

Aldrick turned away. They had come all this way for nothing. A war was soon to begin and they were now in the middle of nowhere, with no upper hand.

Just as he was contemplating forcefully waking Aru for information, she groaned. He turned to see her with open eyes.

Sinin aimed his crossbow down at her.

"Greetings, old friend," he said bitterly.

Aru didn't respond. Her attention locked on Aldrick and a faint yet strikingly malevolent smile sprouted on her face.

"Your doom approaches, little one," she spat. "My

lord will swat you all. You have not the power to stop him. No wielder does."

Télia stooped and gripped Aru by the collar. "Aru, tell us where the Halfstone is. Tell us and you may find some peace in the Life Afterwards!"

Aru snorted. "You truly had hope didn't you—that even after my lord's return to supremacy it still could exist? No, no it was destroyed. He destroyed it." She began to laugh, then spluttered and coughed up blood.

"You're lying," insisted Télia, hiding doubt. "That's not possible."

Aru shook her head. "Wrong. Slowly, over years, the stone oozed my lord's storm. In time he was able to wield once more. He disintegrated the stone from the inside out." She winced. "It... it is dust now."

Aldrick's head dropped. He knew Aru spoke the truth. Télia let her go and walked away, wiping an arm across her forehead. Sinin let out an angered cry and released an arrow into Aru's heart. She became limp. Aldrick shut his eyes. He felt sick and empty. There was a harrowing silence.

"So, what now?" Kaal asked eventually.

"Nothing has changed," said Sinin obstinately. He pulled his arrow from Aru and wiped it down. "War is coming and we must fight. I will be on my way to Galdrem presently. I suggest you all ride at my side, especially Al. He is needed."

"No," said Télia. "Jon was adamant that Aldrick must possess the Halfstone if he were to confront Malath. To chance a victory without it is foolishness. Aldrick deserves no part in this."

Aldrick remembered speaking with Jon before his departure. He had promised Jon that he would not press any further without the stone. However, his mind remained torn. Deep within him, a hatred for Malath seethed, and a longing for vengeance. He wished to see the putrid wielder dead before him! But he couldn't allow hate to conquer him. He had felt it too often recently. It didn't feel natural. He couldn't let it put Télia or his brother in harm's way. They would undoubtedly follow him on whatever road he chose to take from here. Maybe it was best he flee—return to Rain and take them and his family across the sea to safety. And, in truth, he wanted not to break his promise. He knew Jon was terrified that the son of the two he had once so dearly cherished and wished to protect might also perish. He owed it to Jon to run now. Then again, perhaps he owed the Narathlands more...

"Al may do as he pleases—all of you may—but I am going to Galdrem." Sinin made to leave.

"Sinin, wait," Télia went after him. "Keep safe, won't you. Leanne and Flynn need you more than any battle does."

Sinin smiled. "I will be with them soon." He embraced Télia then, after a nod to Aldrick and Kaal, left.

"Leanne and Flynn... they are his wife and son?" For some reason Aldrick had never considered that Sinin might have a family.

Télia nodded. "Yes. I know them well."

"They live in Galdrem? Then why did he leave

them to protect me when he knew Malath was in the city?"

"Because he is a foolish aera who does as he is told," grumbled Télia.

"And you—you have family too. You must wish to see they are safe. Kaal and I will come with you to Daraki' Anya, if you like. They can come south with us. We could all leave these lands."

Télia's face turned a ghostly white and she hurried away.

"Télia!"

Kaal came to his side. "I think you had better go after her, Brother."

Aldrick did, hesitantly. He didn't know what he had said wrong and didn't want to make things worse.

When he emerged from the fort he couldn't see her. De'ama remained with the other horses, waiting patiently outside the watchtower. Hearing a sound he looked up. Télia had opened a hatch at the top of the tower and was climbing through it. He pursued her. When he came out onto the roof he found her with her back to him, staring out across the shadowy plains. Her long hair was caught in the breeze. She sang the same gentle song she had at the border of The Lonely Province. He quietly went to her side. Below them, Sinin travelled down the snaking path to the foot of the mountain.

Télia turned to him. There were tears in her emerald eyes.

"Télia, I'm—"

"My family are dead, Aldrick."

He stared at her. "They... no, no you don't know that."

"You don't understand." She wiped the tears from her eyes. "They died many years ago, when I was nine. Bandits attacked us on the road to Galdrem."

Aldrick took her into his arms. She buried her face in his shirt and wept. His heart was shattered for her. "Télia, I'm..." There were no fitting words. He held on and let her tears flow.

After a time, Télia withdrew her body, looked despairingly into his eyes, then left him upon the roof.

The three of them sat at the base of the tower. It was too hot in the sun and too gloomy in the fort. Aldrick did have half a mind to explore the place but the scent of rotting flesh wafting from one of the passages had dissuaded him. Much of the fort's interior had been cleared out anyway. Malath and Selayna hadn't planned on returning any time soon.

Kaal was busy sharpening a knife—something he often did when he was feeling stressed or uneasy. Télia sat in silence, as did Aldrick, though he was anything but calm. Again, he was attempting to weigh what the wisest course of action to take next was. He kept trying to justify venturing to Galdrem and attacking Malath, but every time he played out the confrontation, it ended with him as a bloody corpse and the others no better off. Heading south was looking to be the better option. He only wished Jon wasn't in Galdrem, set upon defending the lands from Malath. It would surely end dismally for him.

Aldrick wondered what his parents might have done all those years ago, had they not possessed the Halfstone. Would they still have gone up against Malath, or would they have chosen to shelter those they could? He wished that they were here now—here to show him the way.

Suddenly he remembered something that brought with it a small sense of comfort. He rummaged in his travel bag and pulled out the journal Jon had given him before they left the ranges—his father's journal. He carefully opened it at the beginning. Flaky pieces of charred paper fell into his lap. The first pages had been completely ruined by the fire. He continued through until their content became somewhat discernible. They were filled with faded sketches of peculiar plants and objects, many of which were accompanied by lengthy annotations that Aldrick was unable to read. A few, he could, though many words were unknown to him. He didn't mind. It was calming enough just looking at his father's work.

On a page only a little beyond the one he had first opened to in Jon's home was what appeared to be a map. There was a location marked on it, and a single word: 'Cave'. This wouldn't have captured Aldrick's attention, had it not been accompanied by another sketch of a small stone. The stone had lines around it, as if to show that it was emitting something. Light perhaps? It brought to mind Jon's first description of the Halfstone: "A peculiar luminous stone". This must be his father's record of finding it! Underneath the sketch were two more small words that made Aldrick's excitement escalate: 'Green stones'. He jumped to his feet.

"What is it?" Télia asked, standing also.

Aldrick handed her the journal and pointed to the sketch. "Look. My father found more than one of those stones. There must be more, he just never told anyone." Télia put a hand across her mouth. He looked at her directly. "Télia. The map. Do you know where that place is?"

She studied it for a moment. "Yes, I know that area. It is at the feet of the Mountains Nemduran, to the north."

Kaal came to them. "What's going on? Are we off somewhere?"

Aldrick grinned. "Yes we are." He took Télia by the arms. "Can you show us the way?"

She grinned back at him. "Of course I can."

13

THE SYNOD'S SANCTUARY

The outer wall of the city loomed forebodingly. He had long remembered it as a wondrous spectacle, but now he felt only dread for what might lie beyond. How ruthless had Malath and his followers been?

After having travelled along Old Capital Road for the entirety of the way here, Jon now veered off. He did not wish to be seen approaching the main gate. Though there was no sign that it was guarded, he couldn't take any chances. Aeras could be stationed there, or lurking nearby. He had to enter the city a different way. He dismounted at a farmer's stables then continued on foot across fields to the base of the wall, a few hundred paces from the gate. After a quick glance to ensure no one was about, he drew his staff and touched it against the rough stone. He closed his eyes and summoned his storm. It coursed within him and began to flow with ease. He felt wafts of heat as the stone began to melt before him. Slowly, it ran like honey to the ground. Soon a dark street came into view.

When the fissure was large enough to fit through, Jon cooled the stone, stooped and cautiously made his way to the other side. He peered around. This street he remembered well. An old friend had once resided in the lodging ahead of him. He looked for signs of occupancy but there was no light beyond the windows. A number of the surrounding dwelling's windows were lit but fewer than was comforting. People feared that promoting their presence would provoke invasion. The city was grasped by a silent unease. With his staff at the ready, Jon proceeded up the street.

Before he reached the grand marketplace, he made a right turn onto a narrow walkway which led between stores to the sprawling Nobelia district. Its prim streets would see him to the steps of the Synod's tower. Sinin had said that last he knew, Devéna and fellow members of the Synod were taking refuge in the sanctuary of the tower's tallest turret. He must reach it. He needed to know that they were safe, that they were strong and ready to confront Malath.

Jon arrived at the tower in due course, having passed only two citizens on his way, both of whom had eyed his staff warily and let him go by without words. No doubt they feared he was one of Malath's cowardly followers. This was good—it meant that they would be less inclined to pronounce his presence. His anonymity was invaluable.

The tower stood as tall and magnificent as ever it

had, though its prestige was marred by the corpses of two sentries outside the entrance. They must have lain there for days; a foul whiff hung in the air. Squinting up, Jon saw light emanating from a window somewhere at the summit of the tower. He was cautiously hopeful. Somebody was up there.

As his gaze fell, an ever-so-slight movement in the darkness of a nearby street seized his attention. He froze. The beast's eyes gave it away. It was a ka-zchen. He turned, as calmly as he could, to face it. It was crouched low, slinking silently toward him—a shadow in the shadows. In the instant Jon lifted his staff, the beast leaped at him. Though it came down upon him with tremendous speed and strength, the beast's claws fell short of their target. His warding wall was unyielding. It reeled back, scowling. Jon seized this brief moment of reprieve to wield a shard of ice at the head of his staff. While the beast braced itself for a second attack he sent the shard hurtling through its thick skull.

The ka-zchen collapsed to the ground, dead. Jon stooped and took a succession of deep breaths. As brief as the battle was, it had almost been too much for him. Many years had passed since he last strayed upon one of those vile creatures. Its presence in this city he recalled as vibrant and peaceable was most unsettling.

After lingering a moment to be sure the confrontation hadn't alerted any other nearby enemies to his presence, Jon proceeded up the steps into the tower. The golden antechamber was dim and deserted, as was the stairwell. The many candles that lined the circular walls were unlit. Signs of disruption were all around. Large book cases and parchment cabinets had been toppled. Various ornaments lay strewn across the ground. The most prominent wall paintings had been either slashed or burnt where they hung.

With his staff before him, Jon cautiously began to climb the twisting maroon stairs. It would be foolish to presume no one skulked in the shadows above, waiting to strike. This proved not to be the case, however. Soon enough he had reached the Chamber of Deliberation. He paused and took several more deep breaths. The stairs had almost bested him too. His back ached terribly.

The door to the chamber was slightly ajar. After healing himself, Jon pushed it open from afar. It creaked loudly. He froze, fearing he had compromised his position. Nothing stirred. He kindled a flame and went forth. In front of him, the lelylan-wood chairs of the elder wielders' stood empty. Upon the carpet at their feet, bodies lay. There were three, all of them wrapped in drapery from the wall. Jon felt fury take him. Malath was to pay for this villainy!

It was a small comfort knowing some caring soul had sought to rest the bodies in what respectable way they could.

He had to go on. The sanctuary was one level higher. He made toward a small stairwell which led to it but found a warding enchantment blocking his way. This was an encouraging sign.

"Devéna, are you up there?" he called out.

There was a moment of silence before a stern male

voice replied. "Who approaches?"

"My name is Jon. I have come to assist the Synod."

There was another pause, then shuffling. Jon found he was now free to proceed. Smears of blood stained the indigo stairs, diminishing his optimism.

"That is quite far enough." A tall, willowy wielder stood at the head of the stairs, brandishing a staff.

Jon stopped and coolly lay down his own. "Peace, friend. I am on your side. I am no follower of Malath the Wicked's."

The wielder cautiously lowered his staff and stepped aside. "Very well. You may enter our sanctuary... unarmed."

"So be it." Jon left his staff on the stairs and continued.

As he walked through the doorway, Jon was glowered at through large, round spectacles. He recognised the face from many years ago but could not recall a name.

The sanctuary appeared before him as a lord's living quarters. To the left was a roaring fire, set in a wall of polished marble. Before this was a spacious seating area of the most eloquent armchairs and daybeds. The pelt of a ka-zchen lay sprawled on the ground at their feet. Ahead of him was a grand dining table, upon which were many empty wine bottles and platters of half-consumed roast meals.

Jon's eyes fell upon two figures at the far end of the table. One of them was Devéna. She was safe. He felt a heavy weight lift from his chest.

"Devéna, dearest." He strode to her with open arms.

Her companion swiftly stood and blocked his way. "Who are you?"

"It is all right, Frade," said Devéna, rising. "Jon here is a long lost friend to us all." She looked upon Jon warmly and opened her own arms. "Oh Jon, how many years has it been?"

They embraced.

"Many more than too many," he replied, holding her close. Her body felt frailer than he remembered. Of course, it would have been foolish to expect otherwise; her hair was greying when last he saw her, all those years ago.

"Are you well?" he queried. "I saw blood on the stairs and feared the worst."

"I am fine." Devéna gestured to the tall wielder who remained by the door, watching him. "Ferven was wounded when Malath visited last week but is healed now."

"Malath." Jon gritted his teeth. "What he has done is unspeakable. I travelled here with haste."

Devéna smiled.

"We are thankful," she said, gazing upon him. "It seems news does not escape you, even far south in your remote dwelling."

"Aeras brought with them a first-hand account of his presence in Galdrem."

Devéna looked puzzled. "Aeras?"

"Yes—come for young Aldrick."

Her eyes brightened. "Isobel and Gilthred's child! It is splendid to hear he is guarded. I had feared the aeras would not find him."

"Am I to suppose you have news of this wielder, then?" inquired Ferven. "Has he accompanied you here?"

"No, he..." Jon paused. Not everyone here he knew, or trusted. "Young Aldrick is attending to matters," he said tersely. "He may come or he may not. I would not pressure him."

Ferven glared at him. "Are you mad?! You should not have offered him choice when his ability is paramount for any hope of victory. This should have been overseen by one more competent than yourself."

Now Jon was mad. "You speak as if you stand in Devéna's stead. You speak as if you are the Reverend Wielder!"

Ferven's glare turned into an acutely smug smile. "Actually, I am."

Jon turned to Devéna in disbelief. "What? Him? He is the Reverend now?!"

Devéna nodded. "Yes, I have long since given up the title. Ferven was my obvious replacement. He is a most distinguished member of the Synod."

Jon rounded on Ferven. "Much of this makes sense to me now. It was your decision to barricade yourselves in this sanctuary. Tell me, how many days have you been here, letting evil skulk through your city? You should be ashamed!"

"It was hardly my decision," Ferven retorted. "It is written in the old scripture that the elder wielders are to remain here in the event of such ruinous circumstance..."

"And do nothing?! Would you stand idle and see

197

the world collapse around you?"

"No, I would not. I have been spending time diligently considering the most appropriate course of action."

Jon flung his hands in the air. "Oh, so that's what you've been doing all this time—considering things! Do you not realise that the *only* reason you still breathe is because Malath hopes you will align yourselves with him?" He pointed a finger at Ferven's staff. "Your little warding enchantment would not have stopped him entering this sanctuary had he wished you dead." He heaved a sigh. "I am afraid Malath is playing a very devious trick on you, and you are playing straight back into his hands."

Ferven didn't offer a reply. His jaw was firm, his nostrils flared. Jon didn't care for what the fool was thinking, so long as he had absorbed some small sum of reason.

"What is it you think we should do?" Devéna asked Jon calmly.

"I think we must face Malath—gather whatever strength we have and storm Delthendra. We must use this time for retaliation, before it is too late."

Ferven began to laugh.

"Face Malath!" he exclaimed. "You wish death to befall us all, don't you wielder?!"

"No, I simply wish for those who have the power to do something, to do so." Jon strolled to the window and looked down at the city below. Death and despair would soak its streets if nothing was done soon. Truthfully, he hoped Aldrick would abandon all plans to confront Malath, whether he had found the Halfstone or not. It wasn't his responsibility. It was the Synod's... it was his own.

Jon turned. "I am going to Delthendra tonight, with or without your aid."

"Jon." Devéna came to him and seized his hand.

He looked upon her with affection. "What else is there to do?"

She stared into his eyes for a moment, then sighed and rested her forehead against him.

"I will accompany you," said Frade, rising from an armchair. "I have been held up here too long, and not for any good reason."

Jon nodded. "I appreciate it."

Ferven was fuming.

"Fine!" he snapped. "Go with this wayward wielder if you wish, but you won't be welcome back. This sanctuary is for those who want to live."

Jon ignored Ferven's words.

"What will you do?" he asked Devéna. "If you wish it, you should flee this city and take with you those you hold dear."

She shook her head. "No, I will follow you, Jon. You were always wise and I think you are quite right—we should use the time we have to fight back, not hide. Tonight may well be our last opportunity to do so."

"Very well," said Jon. "We must leave right away. Do not forget your staffs."

Ferven watched them with a deadly frown as they walked past him. There were no words of farewell. It was apparent that Devéna and Frade had also resented the Reverend Wielder's handling of this calamity, though they had refrained from expressing it. They were relieved to now be turning their backs to him. There was no rejoicing as they made their way down the tower, however. Devéna shed tears over the bodies which lay in the chamber. It was she who had covered them. One was her younger brother. Ferven had declined a traditional burial as it would have required them to leave the tower.

They exited from the main entrance guardedly. The body of the ka-zchen lay in a heap where Jon had slain it. Black blood oozed from its head and crept between cobblestones down the slope of the street. Thankfully, it appeared that no more of the beasts had been drawn to its scent.

The city was silent. Even fewer windows were lit than before. Midnight had come and gone. Jon could hear himself breathing as they made their way along the dim and deserted streets.

Soon they had passed through the gateway to Akimr Gully. It would offer them a sheltered passage between the sharp roots of the mountains to the very doors of Delthendra. The lelylan trees which grew on either side of the path stood much taller than Jon recalled. Hundreds of dazzling yellow fireflies danced around their clumps of strap leaves as the wielders stole beneath.

Before one final corner which hid the lyceum from view, Jon signalled to halt and turned to his companions.

"Well, this is it," he said. "We must tread as half-moon shadows. If we are outnumbered, which is likely the case, catching the enemy unprepared is our sole advantage. We can only pray that no aeras sense us approaching."

They continued on. The great courtyard came into view. It was cold and still. Upon the ground, dark shapes lay scattered in the pale light—bodies, many of them. With aching hearts the trio meandered between them. They were the lyceum's aera staff, but also, a number of young wielders lay amongst them, dressed in their novice robes. Jon fought to stow his fury. Devéna's hand covered her mouth. She looked close to losing her balance.

"I cannot believe it," uttered Frade in a broken voice.

Jon fixed his attention upon the entrance way. The door was ajar. Monsters lurked within the walls beyond, those willing to take the life of their own young. There was no pity to be felt for any of them.

He seized Devéna's arm and held her steady. "Are you ready?"

She nodded.

"All right, we do this as one."

They stood in a line, staffs raised in front of them, and marched forth. A powerful warding enchantment attempted to restrict passage but it would not withstand them. The vigour of their storm in unison overcame it. They proceeded into the vestibule, which was a mess. Parchment and scrolls scattered the floor. Blood was spattered on the flame-lit walls. The smell of death tainted the air.

Out of nowhere a streak of flame collided with their warding wall, enveloping it for a second before burning out. Devéna whirled her staff and stone roofing collapsed down upon the attacker—a burly wielder in an ill-lit corner. The life was crushed from him.

From inner passages the sounds of alarm broke out—shouting, scuffling.

"Come on!" called Jon. There was no longer any call for discretion.

They emerged into the main hallway. About ten opponents stood in their path.

"Conflagration!" he bellowed.

Together, they wielded a rampant flame and sent it flooding forward. It engulfed the hallway like a broken wave. There were cries as it smothered bodies. Not all were overcome. Counter attacks came as ice, fire and arrows. The trio's line was broken as they fought to evade. To his right, Jon saw Frade's staff split apart and his robes catch alight. He made to help but suddenly found his own staff torn from his grasp. An overwhelming power knocked him off his feet. He was flung through the air and collapsed at the foot of the stairs at the far end of the hallway. Devéna and Frade landed by him. Gravity held their bodies against the ground. Jon peered up. At the top of the stairs stood a figure clad in leather boots and deep purple robes. As it began to trudge down toward Jon, the man's odious face came into view. It was Malath Jayther. Jon urgently tried to find his feet but was incapable of doing so.

Malath watched him with a pretentious smirk.

"Give in, old fool," he demanded. "Before me your head belongs against the ground. I am your lord, returned to power and glory."

Jon snorted. "Glory? You know nothing of it, Malath. Look around you, do you see any glory here?"

Malath's gaze skimmed the hall then set on him again.

"Do I know you, wielder?" he asked, frowning. "Yes, I recall now—you were a member of the Synod."

"Indeed I was," professed Jon.

"And were you not at Darkna the day..." Malath's words trailed away.

"The day you lost your storm?" Jon inserted viciously. "The day your futile attempt to gain the Shard of Heart's Storm failed? Yes, yes I was."

Two more figures appeared behind Malath. One Jon recognised as Selayna, young as ever. The other was a stout wielder with a rough and dark look who was only vaguely familiar.

"What is happening?" asked Selayna, staring down at them with wild eyes.

"Defiant ones," Malath replied over his shoulder.

The stout wielder was glaring at Jon.

"You... I know you!" he cried. "You killed me!" He made toward Jon but Malath raised a hand.

"Now, now, Dron. These timeworn wielders, I yet hope, will see reason and submit. They will bear witness to the cleansing tomorrow. If, then, they still refuse to bow before me, you may have reprisal."

Dron stepped back. He was visibly enraged but

would not dare challenge his master. Jon recognised him now. He had been at Darkna all those years ago. The witless swine had fallen at his very own hand.

"You know we will never surrender, Jayther," cried Devéna from where she lay.

Malath sighed. "Many of your friends have already, Devéna. I see no reason why you need be more foolish than them. After all, you are a wise member of the Synod, are you not?"

"Wisdom—another thing you know nothing of," Jon said through gritted teeth.

The corner of Malath's mouth twitched. "Bold words uttered from such a demeaning stature," he sneered, then opened his arms. "But come, you may stand if you will."

Jon found he was now free to find his feet. He helped Devéna up, then Frade. Frade staggered a little. He sported burn wounds from the battle.

"Let me heal you, my friend," Jon said, holding him steady.

"No," Frade replied stubbornly. "I am capable."

Jon returned his attention to Malath, who watched them with a condescending smile still smeared across his face. The heartless wretch knew not of the haunting sorrows he had sown.

"You are going to pay for this!" Jon yelled. "For everything!" He fought back tears of grief.

Malath sighed again. "Please don't think to try anything more. You will find yourself confined." He drew a staff from his belt and tapped the moonstone tip.

Jon put out a hand and felt a steadfast warding wall. "So you plan to keep us ensnared here like pests, do you?"

"Oh, not right here. I'm sure I can find a more suitable side room in which to secure you." Malath took a step toward Jon. "Know that I regret having to do this, but I must. You brought it upon yourselves."

Though he sounded sympathetic, Jon knew Malath's words were as hollow as his soul. He made no response. There was little to be said now. They were defeated. Malath was more powerful than ever before. Truly, he hoped Aldrick would not come, that he was on his way south with the others. Any steps he took toward Malath were steps toward his doom.

Before taking the three to a small, disorganised study, Malath revived a number of his fallen followers using his unearthly ability to flout death. The wielder's ghostly souls materialised above their bodies before eagerly reclaiming them. Their hearts rekindled promptly. They rose, bewildered for a brief time, then fell to the floor again—kneeling before their lord and saviour. Jon watched, feeling both wonder and anguish. Nothing was achieved in coming here. This had been his decision and it failed dismally. He had failed everyone he ever cared for. Had he travelled directly to Darkna, he could have at least warned the Shard's guardian of Malath's forthcoming arrival. But no, instead he was here—paying the price for his foolishness.

14

THE CAVE

The last of the fire's embers glowed softly at the centre of its ashen bed. Kaal was snoring quietly against one of the nearby trees. Aldrick stood with his back to her, staring beyond their lofty trunks into the sleepy, moon-kissed surroundings. He seemed ill at ease. His fists were clenched.

It was admirable that he was here, that he had not abandoned this quest. She liked that he cared, that he had burdened his shoulders with a heaviness he needn't have taken on. He was one who sought to deal justice where it was deserved. He was one who could be relied upon, trusted. Being in his presence was calming. In past days, he had looked out for her and aided her equally as much as she had him. Of course, it was no secret that he had certain feelings for her. The funny thing was that it was no longer a well-kept secret that these feelings were shared. She had allowed him close to her, even sought comfort in him. She could not call these feelings familiar, however. Romance was not something a novice aera was advised to dabble in, let alone fall into. It wasn't meant to happen, especially with one's own wielder! She was to remain a loyal bodyguard and a watchful companion, nothing more. Now though, she desired to be with Aldrick in other, more intimate ways.

She stood, keeping her travel blanket close to her shoulders, and went to his side.

"Hello Télia." He greeted her warmly, hiding his qualms.

"Hi," she replied.

For a while the two of them just stood there, finding peace in each other's presence.

"I'm sorry. I never realised," he began, but didn't finish his sentence. He was looking upon her with those sincere eyes.

It was the death of her parents he spoke of. No more had been said since she told him of their early passing at Fort Blackbed yesterday. She wanted to reply, but words felt an effort to utter. Instead she rested her head against his shoulder and closed her eyes, then smiled to herself, pleased that thoughts of her occupied his mind, among all else.

"What do you think will become of us?" he asked after a moment of stillness.

She didn't want to think about it now.

"Whatever is meant to," she whispered.

"I guess so."

When no more words came, they settled themselves down beside one another to rest until dawn.

Tomorrow they would continue the search for a halfstone.

The morning songs of many birds woke them. Flocks were congregated in the shelter of the canopy high above their camp. The air was cool and smelt of strawberry plants. Wild ones crept through the tangles of grass, some still bearing pink and white berries.

They had arrived in the area at the fall of dusk yesterday and, so far, only managed a brief scout of the immediate surroundings in search of the cave. It was surely close by, though so too were numerous gullies and crevasses that could be hiding its entrance. So long as they were thorough, it was only a matter of time before they found it.

"Perhaps we ought to split up," Kaal suggested after a lean breakfast.

This was a reasonable idea, she thought. "Yes, but do not stray further than your voice can reach. We haven't the time to lose anyone." Based on Sinin's words, she estimated that today was the day Malath Jayther would make an attempt for the Shard of Heart's Storm. From here, Darkna was at least a full day's ride away. They could only pray that Malath would not be hasty to carry out his murderous ambitions.

After seeing to their horses' contentment, they each set off in a different direction. Kaal went downhill to search along the banks of a river; Aldrick toward a nearby gorge which they had espied yesterday. Télia ventured further up the mountain, hoping to find a vantage point to examine the area in the light of day.

Here and there, great pillars of bedrock jutted from the ground, many overshadowing the surrounding trees. She chose one that offered stable footholds and climbed it to its crest. The view from the top was breathtaking. For leagues ahead of her the countryside was lower than she. Although morning mist blanketed much of it, the highest hilltops were left free to breathe. They appeared as islands in a calm, white ocean. Here, the world seemed at peace—an illusion she knew did not hold in the province of Galdrem. She returned her gaze upon the mountainside. In the distance, she could see Aldrick making his way into the jaws of the gorge. It looked to be a narrow and damp place. Her eyes followed its meandering walls into the mountains. It led from the base of a sheer limestone cliff. This was strange, for a stream trailed from the gorge's mouth into the river below. Where had the water come from…? Underground! Aldrick was heading right for the cave! Excitement brewed in her. She clambered down and hurried to catch up with him—they would find the entrance together.

Aldrick was well into the gorge when she reached him. His attention was occupied by a lively black fantail that flitted around in the air a short way ahead of him. He turned in alarm upon hearing her footsteps but smiled when he saw it was her.

"It is showing me the way," he said cheerfully, gesturing to the bird.

"Yes, your path is true."

He looked a little surprised. "How do you know?"

She brushed one boot through the water. "This stream comes from nowhere."

He nodded in understanding. "Ah… we'll see about that."

They followed the gorge for a further few minutes until the cliff face loomed ahead of them. The gorge widened significantly at its base, allowing daylight in. Green ferns claimed the ground, taking advantage of both the light and the sediment-rich soil. Within these ferns, a number of deer and goat skeletons lay—likely the result of misplaced steps in ill weather. Somewhat ominously, they now adorned the opening of a vast, black void in the mountainside. As Télia had supposed, the stream flowed from within.

"We've found it!" she cried delightedly.

They spontaneously hugged one another. This felt like their first victory in a while.

"Come on." Aldrick entered the cave, igniting a flame above his palm to light the way. She followed. Something felt strange. Yet, it wasn't strange at all; it was very familiar, only more intense. A wealth of storm dwelled within the darkness, somewhere far below them. It must be coming from halfstones!

"Aldrick, watch your step," she cautioned, noting that the ground beneath them was wet stone.

The water was springing from a small crevice in one wall of the cave. Beyond it, a wide passage trailed downward, spiralling into the blackness. It had probably been carved by the water many years ago when it took a different course.

Glow worms shone in the ceiling ahead of them, each one a distant star in a midnight sky.

"I hope those aren't the 'stones' my father mentioned," Aldrick said, gazing up at them.

She shook her head. "No. There are halfstones here. I feel them."

"Look!" Aldrick pointed up at the worms, at something else which glowed faintly green amongst them. It was a small fragment of halfstone.

She couldn't help but squeal. "Yes!"

Aldrick peered around. "I see no pieces of a decent size."

"Well, it has been twenty years since your father was here. The obvious ones may have since been snatched by adventurers or wandering hunters."

"We'll have to go further in." Aldrick stepped forward.

"Careful...."

He slipped. Télia watched in horror as his head struck stone and his body became limp. He began to slide away from her. She launched herself forward and grabbed his leg. Now she was being pulled with him. It was pitch black. His flame had died. Frantically she searched for something to grab hold of and save them both. Her arm struck a jutting boulder and she latched on to it. In the same moment the ground beneath Aldrick's body disappeared. Now he was hanging, saved from falling only by her grasp.

"Aldrick, wake up," she pleaded. "Come on, use your storm, idiot." He didn't respond. "Kaal... Kaal!" Her grip was weakening. Slowly, he was pulling away from her. "No. No, I won't let you go! I won't let you, Aldrick. No!!"

He fell from her.

She closed her eyes. Seconds passed. The sound of his body landing didn't come. She covered her mouth and screamed. This couldn't be... this couldn't be his end. What had she done?!

For a long time she remained there, praying that she would suddenly hear Aldrick shouting to tell her that he was all right. He didn't. An abyss was opening inside her heart.

"Aldrick..."

She was alone now.

With feeble care, she crawled back to level ground and found her feet. She turned one last time and stared blankly back into the darkness. There was nothing, just the indifferent sound of the water flowing by her. She left.

Kaal's face drained the moment he saw her approaching. She must have appeared the ruin she was.

"What has happened?" he asked nervously.

She stood in front of him, light-headed and shaking.

"Kaal..." she began. "Your brother... he fell."

15

AASHKARA

They were in the courtyard. The early sun hid behind stone. The air was still and cold. In a far corner, a mound of black ash and bones smouldered—remains of the bodies which had lain upon the ground last night.

Malath had them on a cart at one end of an orderly line of his followers who stood aside their horses, ready for travel. Selayna and Dron were among them. A regal black stallion waited before the line, master absent—he remained indoors. The courtyard was seized by a foreboding silence. Something was about to happen. Jon had a faint idea of what it might be that chilled his blood.

Devéna clasped his hand. Her face was pale and her breaths deep.

"Jon," she whispered. "I am glad to be in the company of such an old and dear friend today."

He looked into her eyes, tears welling in his own.

He managed a smile but could not speak. Guilt stifled him. She was here because of him.

Malath emerged from the demeaned doors of Delthendra. He strode toward the centre of the courtyard, his face deadpan. Behind him, a large object levitated—part of the elongated backbone of a massive creature. Jon heard Frade gulp beside him and shared the sentiment. This was the dawning of a great evil.

With care, Malath settled the bone upon the ground then distanced himself from it. Everyone watched and waited with baited breath. Malath raised his hands before him and lowered his head in concentration. Slowly, the ghostly smoke of a dragon's soul appeared, enveloping the bone where it lay. It was simply colossal. There were gasps, even fearful cries. Horses whinnied and shifted about fretfully. Little by little, the soul became more vivid, until it was transparent no longer; it was a wholly formed entity, sheathed in sharp, blood-red stone. It lay with its head bowed behind one horned wing, dormant.

Malath lowered his hands and took further steps back, evidently awestruck by the enormity and direful nature of what he had resurrected before him. Every horse, save for his own, broke free from restraint and galloped wildly down the path toward the city. A number of his followers made to flee also but fell as Malath tore their hearts from their chests.

"Traitors!" he bellowed.

The dragon was breathing, slowly and steadily, like waves that washed then subsided from a winter shoreline. It awakened, raising its head and opening smouldering yellow eyes. They fixed on Malath, who nodded in acknowledgement of its attention.

"I live once more because of you, wielder... you have my gratitude." The dragon spoke as thunder would if it had a voice.

"Don't mention it," Malath replied in a notably smaller voice than usual.

The mighty creature stood and spread its wings. The ground shuddered and the courtyard became as dark as the night. It braced its hind legs against the ground and launched its colossal body into the air. Violent gusts of air swept across the courtyard as it ascended into the pallid sky. For a time the dragon glided in broad circles, then roared ferociously and swooped down upon the roof of Delthendra. When it landed, cracks appeared in the chiselled rock and loose stones began to cascade down the sharp walls of the gully. After they had settled, a long silence ensued in which the dragon simply looked on, ignoring them all as they gaped at it from below. Eventually Malath addressed it once more, speaking in a tone of hesitant authority.

"Aashkara, today I travel to Darkna. We shall converge there together. You must not think to destroy the temple before I arrive, or I may be compelled to return you to the Life Afterwards. For as long as you live, your soul is bound to my storm. Your own storm, however powerful it may be, cannot contest that."

Aashkara leered at Malath through thinned eyes then, without words, launched herself into the air once again and soared over them, disappearing from sight.

Selayna and Dron scurried to where Malath stood, continuing to stare in the direction the dragon had left.

"She truly is a formidable creature!" exclaimed Dron.

Malath lowered his gaze and smirked. "Yes, truly she is."

Selayna did not appear impressed.

"That beast—you will end her once she has served our purpose, won't you, Brother?" she asked.

Malath touched her cheek. "Of course I will, Sister."

There was no doubt in Jon's mind that Malath meant it. He would not allow a creature of such power to exist in a world in which he planned to hold sole supremacy.

In short time the horses which had fled were returned to the courtyard and the procession was on its way to Darkna. Jon remained standing, pacing back and forth in the confines of the cart. After beholding the resurrection of the dragon he was feeling ever more hopeless than before. Yet, his mind went on spinning. He wanted to know what was happening, how things would eventuate. He would not close his eyes when they could still be open.

People eyed the procession timidly as it moved down the streets of Galdrem. They huddled in groups, close to the entrances of shelters in case any harm was wished upon them. In the distance, Jon could see Aashkara perched upon the eastern wall of the city. It was likely that many of these people had witnessed the dragon passing overhead. To those unfamiliar with the fable of dragons, and even to those who were, for that matter, she must have appeared a winged demon.

Up ahead, cries of alarm broke out. Some of Malath's followers were pointing toward the Synod's tower. Jon looked to see an orb of fire hurtling down toward Malath. It was Ferven finally taking action! The fire was short-lived. Malath waved his hand and it dissipated into a cloud of black smoke seconds before striking him. He signalled his company to halt and calmly trotted back to his captive's cart. He leered down at Devéna.

"It would appear I have forgotten about your cowardly leader. Whatever am I going to do?"

Devéna didn't reply, just closed her eyes and turned her head.

"You should end that old fool, my lord," spouted Dron. "Show these human vermin your primacy. Show them a sight before they never see again."

Malath chuckled. "Yes, yes, that is what I shall do."

He drew his staff and pointed it at the tower. With a thunderous crash, the tallest turret imploded and began tumbling to the ground below. There were screams and cries from the onlookers on the street but laughter and applause from Malath's followers. Jon was sickened. He opened his mouth to curse at them but stopped himself, realising that the words he had been about to utter were too revolting to do so in the presence of Devéna. Instead, he sullenly watched the last pieces of the turret falling away.

As Jon's gaze fell, he noticed a figure within a nearby crowd of onlookers who wore an aera's cloak. It was Sinin! He must have returned to Galdrem after checking upon Aldrick. His attention was fixed on Malath, who had turned to reclaim lead of the procession. There was a dagger in his hand. Jon urgently waved his own hand to draw Sinin's attention. Sinin glanced up at him with an expression that told of his deadly intent firmly etched on his face. Jon shook his head, urging him not to proceed. The aera glared back at Malath for a moment, then grudgingly sheathed the dagger. A woman with a young boy in her arms came to his side. He embraced them. Jon waited for Sinin's attention once more, then mouthed the words "Get them out."

Sinin nodded. He turned and quietly ushered his family away.

Jon sat and sighed heavily. One could only pray that there was still a chance for those here in Galdrem. There might yet be time for them to board ships and pursue lives in distant, safer lands. The Sanswords Malath was to resurrect would not willingly follow them across water. Whatever fate was to befall these people, it was not far away. Malath would reach Darkna before the sun's setting and have the untold power he so coveted in his wretched grasp.

16

ILLUMIR

Aldrick's thoughts were fractured by an excruciating throbbing in his forehead. He opened his eyes in a daze. He couldn't see. He was blind! Wait... no. No, he was just somewhere very, very dark. He held one hand to his head and searched for the ground with the other. He couldn't find it. Apparently he was floating... was he dead? The thought terrified him. Was this what death was—an eternity of conscious nothingness? No, that couldn't be right. He was just confused. He began to slowly heal his head wound with storm.

When he no longer felt any pain, Aldrick ignited a small flame in one palm and peered around. He was upside down, suspended a short distance above a rough rock floor. Something floated in the air around him... water! Large blobs of water were drifting slowly and aimlessly about like bubbles. Their source was a steady drip from above. Now he recalled entering the cave.

"Télia!" His voice echoed. No answer was returned.

Looking more closely, Aldrick saw bones strewn across the rock beneath him. How had he come to be suspended above them? It must be storm—some kind of warding wall. It had not stopped him abruptly. Had it, he wouldn't be conscious. For whatever reason, he had been intentionally spared from a fatal meeting with the ground.

Using his own storm, Aldrick propelled himself sideways, keeping his flame alight to guide his way. Soon the vigour of the storm holding him up weakened and he touched down against solid ground. He stood, brushed himself off, then brightened his flame.

He was in a massive, seemingly roofless hollowing beneath the mountains. It was eerie. It felt like a dungeon—bare, cold and hauntingly quiet. He squinted to see beyond the reaches of his flame's light. There was no sign of any wielder who possessed the storm that spared his life. Surely there was something here though, something causing the distortion in gravity. He walked until he found a smooth rock wall and began to follow it. With any luck, he wouldn't find himself back where he started.

In a few minutes Aldrick came to a sharp corner. Around it was a sight that made his heart skip a beat. Jutting from a great mound of pale rock was a seam of remarkably large, luminous green stones. This was the source of the Halfstone his father found all those years ago! Excitement rippled through him. His fall had not been in vain. Perhaps it was these very stones which had caused the distortion in gravity. He assumed they held storm within them now—it was why they illuminated their surroundings in the enchanting way they did.

He made toward them, pausing suddenly as his flame wavered, as if it had been caught in a draft. It did so only momentarily, then continued burning as a sphere again. This was a good sign. If there was a nearby passage that led to the outside world he might not have to find a way back up the crevasse he fell down.

Aldrick continued to the base of the mound encrusting the stones. Its surface was rough and in many places fractured, but looked sturdy enough to take his weight. He clambered to the top where the seam of stones peaked then arced left. Their green glow was so intense that Aldrick no longer had need of his flame. For a while he just stood and gazed upon them. They took the form of stalagmites, only their surface was far too smooth for them to be so. At their core their glow was fiercest. In places, it almost appeared as though there were organic veins running through them.

Hypnotised, Aldrick reached out to touch one. The mound shuddered beneath him. Startled, he stepped back, tripped and tumbled painfully down to the cavern floor. He hurriedly scrambled back, away from the living stone… but it wasn't stone at all. The seam of green flared brighter, revealing the figure of a massive winged creature awakening, unfurling. Aldrick stared in terror. The creature lifted an enormous lizard-like head and opened crystal blue eyes. He gulped; he was about to die horribly.

To show his awareness of total inferiority, Aldrick bowed his head and gave the creature opportunity to do away with him as it pleased. He could feel its eyes firmly fixed upon his puny, trembling figure. Surely a killing blow would come at any moment…

"Human." It was… speaking to him?! It had a deep, grumbling voice—an avalanche of rocks down a mountainside. "You are no human."

Aldrick lifted his head very slightly and looked up to see its own now very close to him, held up by an elongated neck of plated scales. It was surveying him keenly. He opened his mouth as if he was about to speak but no words came out.

The creature retracted its head and appeared to frown. "You are a storm wielder, are you not?"

This time Aldrick was compelled to reply.

"I… I… am, yes," he stammered, remaining huddled upon the ground.

"Peculiar," the creature said musingly. "And why have you interrupted my drowse?"

He frantically racked his brains for an innocuous reply. "I meant not to, oh great… one. I mistook your body for stone. But I see now that you are a mighty and majestic being."

The creature frowned again, and then yawned, revealing jagged fangs and a forked, snake-like tongue.

"Wielder, there is no need to offer me flattering words. I do not intend to harm you," it said plainly.

"You don't?"

"No, for you and I are alike."

"We are?"

"Yes. You and I are storm bearers both. It is rather a shame you aren't a wild creature, though. I find myself peckish." The creature rested its head upon the ground, now seemingly uninspired by his presence.

Aldrick cautiously got to his feet. "You... are a dragon, aren't you?"

It snorted loudly and misty vapour erupted from its nostrils. "Yes—dragon, that is what inhabitants of this world call me."

"Of this world," he repeated. "You are not from this world?"

"No. I come from its moon. Solemn, I believe you call it."

He was dumbfounded. "But... what? How long have you been down here?"

The dragon didn't reply immediately. For a second Aldrick was sure he saw the sad and distant look of reminiscence in its eye.

"For a long time I have been here," it said finally.

Aldrick continued to stare at it. His world had been turned upside down when he discovered he was a wielder, but now, having strayed upon this dragon from another world, his concept of reality was being radically reconstructed. In past days, he had been quietly attempting to mentally prepare himself to witness the dragon Malath revived, but encountering this one down here in the lonely dark was unforeseen and almost inconceivable. Perhaps the most ridiculous thing of all was that he was conversing with it.

The dragon's fiery blue gaze met him once more. "Wielder, you failed to tell me why you are here…"

"I fell down here."

"This was the result of mere foolishness and misfortune?"

"Foolishness, yes, but not misfortune, as it turns out. I was looking for something…"

"What was it you were looking for?"

"I was looking for a piece of the luminous spires which line your back."

The dragon lifted its head and scratched its chin with a razor-sharp claw that extended, along with four others, from one of its front feet. "That is a most peculiar thing to be looking for, wielder. Tell me why."

"Years ago my father found a piece in this cave. A piece that must have broken off of you. I assume you know it withholds storm. I seek a piece so I can trap another wielder's storm inside it."

"That seems like a rather foul and devious thing to do. Why would you wish to do that to a fellow wielder?"

"Because the wielder himself is foul and devious. He thinks of humans as vermin and means to rid the world of them." Aldrick's jaw clenched. "And he murdered my parents."

"Ah, so you are on an errand of righteousness and revenge, then?"

"I am."

"That I can commend, wielder. However, allowing you to leave with a piece of my backbone is something

I am less inclined to condone. As you said, my spires hold storm within them. Storm is my life-force."

"I completely understand," Aldrick replied hastily, fearing he may have angered the dragon. It still appeared quite calm. Its eyes were half closed. He wasn't focused on convincing it to give him anything right now anyway. He was far too fascinated by its mere existence and skyward origin.

"So, you are from Solemn," he began. "Why then have you been here so long in this dark, isolated hollow of the Narathlands?"

"Solemn was my old home, yes," the dragon said forlornly. "I was left here after a disagreement with the king of my kind."

"You were exiled?"

"Yes. We came here many ages ago, bringing with us the remnants of another race of dragons we were in feud with on Solemn. They are vile and depraved creatures that blindly devour and burn storm, rather than endeavour to preserve a natural balance, as my kind does. Our king wanted them gone from our world forever. He banished them beneath the earth here, to be eternally scolded by molten fire and intoxicated by the wealth of storm the heart of this world bears within it. I believed that punishment too pitiless and told him I would not allow it. He was enraged and commanded me to remain here. Though he wished never to see me again, he had heart enough to spare me the hellish fate of our foes."

Aldrick's mouth was half open. He pressed his palms against his temples so that his head wouldn't explode. "Are you telling me that there is an entire race of dragons trapped beneath the surface of this world?"

"Yes, there is."

"Surely it's not possible," he said in awe and bewilderment.

The dragon chuckled in a deep and rather disconcerting way. "A revelation I would not expect such a modest-minded creature to comprehend. I assure you, though—it is the truth."

Aldrick sighed. "Actually, there is much that has come to light recently that I have found difficult to comprehend, and the truth is, I'm becoming somewhat accustomed to it."

The dragon chuckled once more. "I find your company enjoyable, little wielder. Do you have a name?"

"My name is Aldrick," he said. "And what is your name, oh sky dragon?"

"My name? It will hold little meaning to you and sound unpleasant in utterance, so you may call me what you will. Go on Aldrick, give me a name."

He thought for a moment. What could he call a giant, stone-scaled dragon that glowed in the dark? "Well... because you illuminate your surroundings, I will name you Illumir. How does that sound?"

"Illumir," the dragon repeated thoughtfully. "Yes, I like it."

Aldrick felt more relaxed now, though still fairly dumbfounded; he had just befriended a dragon. He had also discovered that, essentially, there was a hellish underworld beneath them. It wasn't the best of news.

Télia and Kaal now came into his thoughts. They were probably searching for him. They might think him dead! He needed to get back to them. Today was the day Malath planned to infiltrate Darkna. He had no idea how long he had been unconscious. It could already be too late! Considering the circumstances, he reasoned they needed this dragon, Illumir, on their side. He could give Malath's dragon a run for its coin. It would undoubtedly be their deadliest foe. He just needed to convince Illumir that there was cause to aid them.

"So, Illumir," he began. "Those vile and depraved dragons you spoke of... perhaps just by mere coincidence, the foul wielder I want to kill has one under his command and is using it to retrieve for himself the power to wage war across these lands."

Illumir's attention was caught. "Nonsense, the few that escaped the banishment were put to death. It is not possible that one still roams the surface of this world." He spoke with apprehension, afraid his words were false.

"It should be impossible, yes. But this wielder can resurrect the dead."

Illumir looked at Aldrick for a moment and then scowled. "This foul wielder of yours is making a momentous mistake. Do you not realise what this means, Aldrick? The dragon will seek to free his kind, and should they escape, they will set this world ablaze."

"There is a way it can free them?" He hadn't really

227

considered this.

"Yes. Lord Wielder Akimr, who ruled when those dragons were brought here for banishment, helped our king forge a seal which was to forever shut the chasm down which they were banish—"

"Hold on, hold on... wielders were involved in this? Then why does no one seem to know anything about it?"

"History can easily be forgotten. I presume Akimr ordered that there be no written account of it, in case someone ever sought to break the seal."

"What exactly is the seal? Was it forged with storm?"

"Yes, a great temple was built at the mouth of the chasm. Into its stone the king infused vast amounts of his storm. If that temple were ever destroyed, the seal would be broken."

Realisation struck Aldrick like a club to the forehead. "Darkna—the temple that stands at the mouth of a mighty chasm! That is where Malath is leading the dragon to gain him access to the power he desires—the Shard of Heart's Storm. That is where it is kept. He doesn't know what he is doing! The dragon will destroy the entire temple! We have to stop it. We have to go there now!"

Illumir rose upon his four armoured legs. "Indeed we must, or else life on this world will be extinguished forever. It appears fate led you here, Aldrick. You need my help, as I needed word of this dragon's return. So long as it is stopped from destroying the temple I can help you defeat your foul wielder, should you ask it of me. However strong his stormpower becomes in unity with this 'shard' you speak of, his body will still snap between my jaws."

"I'm glad you are on our side, but I'm afraid we may be too late. Today was the day Malath threatened to take the Shard."

"Well, by my estimation the day is not yet over, and fortunately, I have wings." Illumir spread his wings to their full span. They were enormous, webbed by thick, leather-like skin, the same white colour as his stone-plated body. Each had five fingers composing its form. At the tips of these, more green spikes protruded and gleamed brilliantly.

For a moment Aldrick simply gaped, then managed a faint "Whoa."

"Come—we must go at once." Illumir strode past him. He followed but maintained a distance so as to avoid being crushed by the dragon's lengthy tail. With every step Illumir took, the ground shook and Aldrick feared the roof would give way above them. Not a pebble fell. The rock that remained after countless years of water erosion was sturdy.

They soon reached the area where Aldrick had woken in the air. It appeared that gravity had returned to normal. The dripping water now reached the bone-strewn ground.

"Illumir, it was you who stopped my fall, wasn't it?" he asked.

"Indeed it was," replied the dragon. "Wild animals often misstep, as you did. I favour my meals fresh." Illumir looked up and grumbled. "Aldrick, will you allow me to carry you?"

"Carry me?" Aldrick wasn't sure if he liked the sound of that.

"Yes—carry you—between my claws," confirmed Illumir. "You needn't be afraid. I have a gentle grasp and will be mindful of your flimsy body."

"Well, all right then."

Illumir raised one of his back feet then, after Aldrick had hesitantly stepped beneath it, closed his claws around him and lifted him off the ground. The dragon then began to scale the nearest wall. For the most part Aldrick kept his eyes closed, dreading that Illumir might forget about him and either let him fall or squish him. Thankfully, neither of these happened and they were soon at the top. The light of the glow worms had vanished in Illumir's wake and the entrance tunnel was instead lit by the dragon's own green flare.

At the point where the stone ceased to slope, Illumir set Aldrick down. "Thanks."

The naked daylight flooding the entrance of the cave was blindingly bright. Aldrick covered his eyes with a hand while they adjusted. Through his fingers he saw a figure approaching. It was Télia. His heart warmed. She froze and let out a shrill scream. He realised she had just seen the most profoundly terrifying thing in all her life, as he had when first beholding Illumir's fearsome majesty.

"Télia, Télia, it's all right. He's friendly." Aldrick went forward and embraced her. "He can help us."

"No, no," she cried. "Aldrick, it's a dragon!" Her breaths were rapid and her eyes frantic.

He grinned. "Yes, that is Illumir."

Illumir took a step toward them and stooped his head.

"Hello, Télia," he said, looking upon her with a smile that was as polite as a dragon's smile could be.

Télia gaped at Illumir for a moment, then her eyes began to glisten and she buried her head under Aldrick's neck. "Aldrick, I thought... I thought I had lost you... but I haven't, and... and now you have a dragon?!"

He stroked her flowing tresses. "I'm here."

A swift arrow sped past them and splintered against Illumir's armoured chest. It had been sent from within a shaded patch of ferns.

Knowing he had forfeited his hiding spot, Kaal stood. His face was as white as snow.

"Y... you two, get away from it," he stammered, beckoning Aldrick and Télia to him.

Illumir's eyes narrowed. "Another human? He is your friend, Aldrick, or shall I devour him?"

Kaal stumbled back and tripped over upon hearing the dragon's words.

"He's my brother," Aldrick said, going to Kaal. "Kaal, it's all right. The dragon is our friend, our ally." He pulled him to his feet.

Kaal stared at Illumir.

"Friend? That's nice," he said blankly.

"Yes, and just as we do, he has pressing reason to reach Darkna. It turns out there is a menace even greater than we knew."

Aldrick hurriedly told Kaal and Télia of the

231

malevolent dragons trapped beneath the chasm at Darkna's feet, and of the likelihood of their imminent release. They seemingly failed to fully grasp what he was saying but this came as no surprise—it sounded ludicrous. It was all truth, though, and this mighty dragon here with them now was the one hope they had left.

"We must make haste," said Illumir once Aldrick had finished speaking. "Aldrick, you and your friends must travel with me."

Aldrick stared up at him. "Travel with you? We can't really do that, Illumir. We don't have wings."

"Yes you do. You will sit on my back. You should find that the gaps between my spires offer a fitting place to seat yourselves. I will fly with caution and ease."

"He wants us to ride on his back?" Kaal asked in a whisper, avoiding eye contact with the dragon.

"It may be the only way," said Télia. "We have very little time and must take the quickest path."

Kaal heaved a sigh. "All aboard, then."

"We must set our horses loose first. De'ama will lead yours to Galdrem."

"Good plan." Aldrick looked up at Illumir. "We won't be long. Will you wait for us here?"

"Of course I will," Illumir said. "Go now, Aldrick, Télia and Kaal. Return with your hearts hardened. There will be only darkness at Darkna today."

They left the dragon and returned to their horses, which were happily grazing by the campsite. Télia uttered soft words to De'ama before setting her on her way.

"Goodbye, chum," Aldrick said, patting Tame on the neck. His steed whinnied, nodded, then left with Stub to join De'ama. The horses carried away with them travel provisions that were no longer necessary.

Before returning to Illumir, the three of them rallied together. Aldrick surveyed Télia and his brother.

"Are you ready for this?" he asked.

Télia didn't respond. She simply stared at him with wide eyes. He knew she was anticipating the coming events at Darkna far more than the airborne journey there.

Kaal shrugged. "What is it people say... 'as ready as I'll ever be'?"

"Right, let's do this."

When they returned they found that Illumir had scaled one wall of the gorge and was gazing out across lands afar. Out in the open, the green colour of the dragon's spires was fainter and it was now his plated white crust that shone fiercely, reflecting the sunlight. He stood a god of creatures.

Seeing them approaching, Illumir clawed his way back down, then lowered one of his wings to the ground, offering a passage to their seats. "Come—let us be on our way."

"You first, Brother," said Kaal, looking at Aldrick with an expression that said "Don't expect this to end well."

After a moment of justifiable hesitancy, Aldrick climbed up Illumir's wing and awkwardly sat himself down between two of the dragon's great spires. There was enough space for Télia to find her way in behind him. She fastened her arms around him and rested her head against his back.

After Kaal had seated himself between the spires behind them, Illumir spread his wings.

"Hold fast," the dragon grumbled. With a mighty thrust he launched his rocky bulk into the air. Immediately, their backs were toward the ground. They clung on for dear life.

Aldrick closed his eyes and willed the tug of gravity to weaken.

"Are you alive back there?!" he called out to Kaal.

"Mostly," Kaal replied. Aldrick almost failed to hear him over the rushing sound of air passing as they rapidly ascended into the sky.

Peering sideways, he saw they were nearing the height of the weatherworn mountain peaks. His eyes followed their path eastward. Somewhere away in the distance Galdrem stood, and beyond—Darkna—their journey's end.

Illumir ceased flapping his wings and for a brief moment they descended in a sharp dive, before the dragon spread them to their fullest span and they transitioned into a swift and steady glide. Hazy clouds passed by above and below them. The ground, when it was visible, looked like an exquisitely detailed picture map. Everything was in miniature but drawn to perfect scale. Aldrick wondered how many people had ever seen the world from such a view, and how many could say they had from upon the back of a dragon while the woman of their dreams held onto them as if there was no tomorrow. Perhaps there would be no tomorrow.

He rested a hand over Télia's. Whatever happened, he could not ask to be in better company. He remained anxious of Jon's fate, however. What had become of him? Would he be there to fight alongside them, or had he already fallen at the hands of Malath? May it not be so. Regardless, with those who remained standing, Aldrick would stand with, and for those who no longer did, he would fight until his dying breath to avenge. He knew now that he would never have had it otherwise. This was his destiny.

17

THE SHARD OF HEART'S STORM

Malath looked beyond the mighty archway. Darkna stood, a towering stronghold, forewarning of the boundless precipice atop which it stood. Beyond the temple's multitude of columns and walls of grim stone, the ultimate prize awaited him. Anticipation was causing his heart to thud like a sledgehammer. He brought his mount to a standstill. So too did his faithful. No one uttered a word. No one would; this was his hour, this was his day, one that had been robbed from him for far too long... but no longer.

The dragon Aashkara, who had been slowly spiralling in the sky above, dived like a bird of prey and perched on the temple's court. It was upon that very court, all those years ago, that Malath's storm had been taken from him. Today he would stand upon it and see history rewritten. The world would behold true power and vision!

Malath signalled to continue and the procession began to ascend the final length of road which led to the court steps. These proved too steep for the horses to climb, so they dismounted. He took his frail and defeated captives from their cart and dragged them up the stairs behind him. In the shadow of Aashkara he set them down so that they could witness the proceedings—see the chamber that sheltered the Shard, the one the Synod believed impenetrable, demolished by his winged puppet.

Malath stooped to address them.

"See me become divine," he whispered.

They didn't respond. This didn't bother him; in fact, it amused him. Their eyes would soon be opened and their heads bowed.

Before directing the dragon onward, Malath strode to the edge of the court and looked down upon the dreary grassland. The remains of the ancient Sanswords' bones lay in a chaotic, but nonetheless collective scattering across the ground. By his hand they would soon live again; an army to end all others; the rebirth of a demised race to decimate another. It was all so very close now.

"Aashkara." He spun on his heel to address her. "The Shard lies within those aged walls. The warding enchantment placed upon its holding chamber is fuelled by its own storm—the deed of a sniffling wielder who agreed to shelter the Shard in exchange for all the comforts of a king. You may find the enchantment sturdy but you will break it, and you will crush the life from the wielder. The Shard does not belong to one so worthless. It belongs to me. Go forth and retrieve it."

Aashkara appeared hesitant. "Wielder, am I to simply believe that you will let me live after I have completed this petty errand for you? What assurance do you offer?"

Malath was infuriated. "I have given you my word. Do you think I would break it?" He stepped closer to the depraved beast. "And do you think you really have any choice? Your life depends on me!"

The dragon's fiery eyes became slits. She scowled, then stormed away toward the temple's entrance. He watched her go, his own eyes narrowed. Had she seen through his words? He couldn't risk her suddenly turning on him, however suicidal that might be for her. Fortunately, he could soon be rid of the monster. Sustaining her life had been a hefty encumbrance, but it was to pay off significantly.

Malath looked to his dear sister. She too eyed the dragon with disdain. He took her hands in his. "All is in order. You need not be vexed."

Selayna's frown faded and she began to giggle. He kissed her cheek, then left to oversee Aashkara's chore.

The dragon stood before the pillared entrance to Darkna's hall. It was far too narrow for her enormous body to pass through, so she thrust one shoulder against the encompassing wall. It was reduced to rubble. This brought to Malath's mind their accord. After uncloaking the Shard, Aashkara was to be free to demolish this temple, pursuing her belief that it would free her kind from the fires beneath them. Though her intent was commendable, it was heartbreaking to think that the dragon held faith in such a profoundly ludicrous myth. He would, in fact, be doing her a kindness in returning her to the Life Afterwards before she had a chance to discover its falsehood.

He cautiously trailed the dragon into the hall, conscious that the wielder in the Shard's holding chamber, at least at present, possessed more power than he. There the chamber stood, at the centre of an otherwise open and bare interior—a room wrought of marble, its doorway flooding torchlight. The wielder appeared as a silhouette inside. To avoid his attention, Malath veered left and concealed himself in a shadowy corner of the hall. From there, he watched Aashkara proceed, with bated breath.

"Surrender yourself, wielder," the dragon snarled as she bore down upon the chamber.

The wielder made no reply. Instead, he raised his staff and began attacking Aashkara with fervent flurries of frost, their intensity extraordinary. For a brief moment her entire body became encased in a thick, transparent shell of ice before, with a deafening smash, she shattered it into a multitude of tiny pieces.

Now in a deadly temper, she engulfed the chamber in a rampant tempest of red fire that floodlit the entire hall. When her breath was ended, black smoke subsided to reveal the chamber undamaged. The walls were not even charred. The wielder inside was chortling.

"You stupid slug, you have no power over me!" he jeered, then prompted two nearby pillars to collapse upon the dragon. She brushed them from her like twigs.

"Fool, your end is me." She began hammering her mighty body against the chamber.

The presence of the warding enchantment became perceptible as ripples across an unseen barrier, a hand's breadth from the marble walls. The wielder continued aggressively attacking Aashkara but, in her wrath, she was irrepressible. Her blows kept coming, causing the entire temple to shudder and rumble. Suddenly there was a thunderous crack as the enchantment broke and the chamber exploded.

Before the stunned wielder could react, Aashkara flicked him away and he became a bloody splodge on a far wall. His staff, carried with him, disintegrated on impact. The power of the Shard was his no longer.

Malath stepped out from the shadows. "Aashkara, you have done well. I am most impressed."

The dragon turned and glared at him. "Well, wielder, what are you waiting for? Come and claim your prize."

He went forth.

"Wait for me outside," he ordered.

She turned and stormed away, leaving him facing a thick plume of dust. With patience absent, he raised a hand and swept it aside. The interior of the chamber was now unlit. The torches which had brightened it were missing, as were the walls on which they had been fitted. Malath looked up. From the ceiling of the hall, six huge oil lamps hung on chains which he ignited to provide light. He found himself amongst total ruin. The floor was a mix of rubble, broken furnishings and various other indiscernible dust-coated objects. In one corner was a circular settee. Upon it, a number of young whores lay dead, crushed by falling marble. Left of this, a bare stone altar stood, upon which the Shard must have rested. Malath went to it and searched the floor at his feet. Though he could not see it, the Shard's stormflow was so potent that he could feel it—a warming breeze passing through his chest. It was very close... there! It lay amongst stray marble blocks a short way away—a rough piece of dark red metal surrounded by tiny, flickering sparks of green. Shivers washed through him. This was it. He stretched out his hand and it came to him. He took it with care but firm intention. Its storm coursed through him and he felt blissful elation. Its power was his! He laughed aloud. All these long years and now here he stood—a god among wielders.

Malath turned to exit the hall and found Dron and his dear sister in front of him. They ogled at the Shard in his hand.

"Oh, Brother, it is yours," Selayna exclaimed.

"What does it feel like, my master?" asked Dron in awe. "I can feel it from here... I can only imagine what it is like to have it in your grasp."

Malath looked down at the Shard. "No, you cannot imagine. It is like nothing else. I am... eternal."

He strode outside. All eyes were set on him. He moved to the edge of the court. Before him, the Sanswords were ready to be arisen. He held the Shard out before him. Now was the time. With all its glorious power in his possession, he found it an effortless task to summon the desert warriors' souls. He willed them to once again be bound by skin and bone. Like winter mist over a lake, they appeared above their skeletal remains then slowly began to reanimate. Once awoken, they roared passionately at the sight of their kin around them.

After boisterous celebrations, the Sanswords turned to Malath and cheered, praising him with hands raised to the sky. Never had he seen these creatures in the flesh. Their kind had diminished long before his time. Gazing upon them now, he was impressed. They stood tall, their bodies armoured with thick plates of sand-toned skin. Their eyes were dark; their hands were talons. They were an army of death.

One—evidently their leader—stepped forth and bowed. They all followed suit. This was what Malath had dreamed of—being looked up to, being revered. Not devalued and treated like simple human scum.

He raised his hands. "Warriors of ages past, breathe the air of a new dawn!"

They roared ever more fervently at this. He signalled for silence.

"I have granted you life. Now, do my bidding and take it from the humans that plague this land, for they are undeserving. No doubt you bear deep resentment of them. Do you not wish rabid revenge upon them for driving you from your homeland? For driving you to extinction? Go now and have it. Begin with their city in the west. Slaughter them all!"

The Sanswords' battle cries were deafening. They

turned and began marching swiftly toward Galdrem. Malath watched them go, feeling wholly powerful.

He turned to his faithful, who had been spectators of the army's awakening. They eyed him now, in silence, nodding their heads in recognition as his gaze crossed them. Dron and Selayna were nearest to him, expressions of admiration upon their faces. His captives remained huddled under his warding enchantment. He bore down on them.

"So will you stand with me, or do you remain blind and foolish?" he asked.

They failed to reply. Malath could see that their hearts were sunken. Perhaps these remaining few truly were a lost cause… perhaps he should be rid of them. No, not yet. He would allow them one final chance. He stood straighter.

"Wielders, no longer are you imprisoned. You may move freely. But choose your actions wisely. Any harm you deal upon my allies, I can reverse in the blink of an eye. I implore you to align yourself with me. It is the wisest choice and it is your only choice."

Devéna shot him a vicious glance.

"Not a chance," she said, stressing every word.

Malath sighed. He held fond memories of this old hag. She had once been his tutor at Delthendra and had avidly supported his bid to become the minister. Now she stood before him, refusing his kindness. She would pay dearly for it, as would her gutless friends.

Just as he had chosen how he would end them—by imploding their rib cages and crushing their organs, Dron stepped forward.

"My Lord, you will let me have my revenge, will you not?" he asked. "That one is mine." Dron pointed at Jon, the insolent wielder who had robbed him of life.

Malath chuckled. "Ah yes, of course Dron. He is all yours."

Dron curled his lip and marched straight up to Jon. He might have looked ominous had he not been half the wielder's height. "For you, there shall be no returning." His voice trembled with hatred.

Jon heaved a sigh of indifference. "Go on then, Dron. May it bring you satisfaction."

"Enough of this triviality," snarled Aashkara. "This temple is mine now. I shall not be kept from destroying it any longer. Deal with those wielders elsewhere."

Selayna turned and looked Malath in the eye. "Yes Brother, must we not *tend* to this dragon before settling other matters?"

"Indeed." Malath raised a hand. "Dron, hold for a moment."

Dron stepped away from the wielder. "Fine."

Malath looked up at the misguided dragon. "Aashkara, go now, see your kin are freed."

Aashkara snorted, then turned and trudged toward the temple.

"Now. Do it now, Brother," Selayna muttered in his ear. "Return that monster to the Life Afterwards."

Malath raised the Shard in his hand... Aashkara stopped in her tracks. He too hesitated. Was she conscious of his deceit? The dragon's head turned, but her attention did not fall upon him. She instead looked out across the sunken land toward the long spine of the

244

Mountains Nemduran. He followed her gaze. There, in the distant sky, was a huge creature flying toward them. It was another dragon! How was this possible? Had Aashkara secretively summoned some accomplice to aid her? Apparently, this wasn't so.

The dragon gasped. "It cannot be."

Malath lowered the Shard.

"Aashkara, what is this?" he demanded.

"I cannot say in certainty," she said. "But it appears you may have need of me yet, wielder. An olden enemy of mine approaches. And, if my keen eyes are not mistaken, he is accompanied by humans, and one of your own kin. I imagine that their cause conflicts not only with my own." She glared at him through fiery narrowed eyes.

The approaching dragon brought with it humans and a wielder? Malath wondered who they could possibly be. If Aashkara was correct in thinking that they had quarrel with him, it was a problem. The powers the Shard gave him were not enough to defeat a dragon whose soul was not already his to toy with. She was right. He still needed her help. This irritated him immensely. It was a complication that wasn't meant to be happening, and how could it be? Where had this dragon come from? Had it traversed the plains of time? It should be dead! It should be fragments of dry bone, dust on the wind! The one fortunate thing was that it was Aashkara's adversary.

"You will kill this dragon if it's the last thing you do," he ordered.

"Indeed I shall," Aashkara replied keenly. "I will

crush him." She braced herself and roared thunderously in its direction.

Everyone was now watching the second dragon approach. There were apprehensive murmurings amongst his faithful few. They were fearful. Dron and Selayna both shot him glances, seeking reassurance. Malath had none to offer. He secured the Shard in a pouch on his belt. With it there, he could safely wield its storm. Somehow that storm no longer comforted him as much as it had. He felt hot and flustered. A drop of sweat trickled from his brow.

18

GAMBLE OF THE FATES

Illumir had not reacted to the dragon's roar. In fact, he had been silent for the entirety of the journey. He was likely harried by uncertainty, and fairly so. They all were. The chasm down which the dragon's foes had been banished loomed ahead—a vast, hazy gouge in the landscape. There, at its edge, towered the temple Darkna. Upon its court the awakened dragon watched them approach. Near it were a number of figures whom Aldrick couldn't identify from afar. Many were wielders though, as they wore robes of various shades. One of them was surely Malath.

It appeared that they were arriving at the eleventh hour. Events had already been set in motion. To their right, Aldrick could see an army shrouded by dust, marching toward Galdrem. Soon it would reach the surrounding villages. They were Sanswords. Their presence told that Malath already had the Shard of Heart's Storm in his grasp. Fortunately, the greater threat to the entire world was yet to be unleashed—the dragon had not yet broken the seal holding its kin at bay. They could only pray that Illumir possessed the might to impede it. It looked much larger than he was.

Malath, Aldrick wanted all to himself. The wielder was to pay for all his villainy! Most of all, he was to pay for taking his parent's lives. He was to pay the dearest price.

Télia's arms tightened around Aldrick. Her body felt cold. He was unsure if this was because of the harsh wind hurtling past, or because she was terrified. He took her hands and warmed them.

Illumir began to descend upon the court. As he neared, Malath's dragon took steps back, but not out of caution. It was merely granting Illumir space to land. Its leviathan face was one of pure loathing. Aldrick glanced at their audience. Jon was among them. His heart jumped. Jon was still alive! And it appeared that he was accompanied by a friend or two! Aldrick raised a hand in greeting. The others in the gathering were not allies. Behind their expressions of awe and alarm was bitterness and blind hatred. This was most telling on the face of a tall, aging wielder dressed in dark purple robes. It was Malath. There was no doubt. He stood as a self-righteous commander would. Aldrick felt a fire suddenly rage inside him, synchronous with a surge of storm. He wanted to attack the worthless murderer right now! But he knew that words must first be shared. There was the safety of his companions to consider also. He hadn't the freedom to be reckless.

Illumir landed lightly, then lowered a wing to allow

them down. Aldrick stood, wielded a warding wall between them and Malath, then turned to Télia and Kaal. "Stay behind me, all right. Promise me you won't go intentionally blundering into harm's way, even if I'm done-in."

Kaal nodded. "Suits me, Brother."

Télia frowned. "Aldrick, I'm your—"

"I relieve you of duty," Aldrick interrupted. "I need you alive more than anything, damn it!"

Her frown became a smile. "You're just an idiot. Why do I even bother?"

He returned her smile, vividly aware that it might well be the last time he was ever able to, then took a breath and made his way down onto the court.

"Aldrick, I will watch over you and your humans," Illumir said calmly. "You must not rely on me, though. My winged foe will keep me from that foul wielder at any cost. If he falls, so does she." His and the red dragon's eyes were locked.

Aldrick nodded. "Thanks, Illumir. You can best her. I know you can."

The dragons now wrathfully bore down on each other and a fierce dispute erupted that sounded like an ocean-born tempest. They took to the skies. Aldrick turned and faced Malath. The wielder stood staring back at him with an expression of puzzlement upon his ashen face.

"You," he muttered, taking steps forward to survey Aldrick more closely. "I know who you are... yes, yes... I can see it in your face. You are the Aedimons' child." He sneered, then turned to address his companions. "It appears this untimely interruption brings with it a small fortune!" he exclaimed. "An opportunity to see Isobel's child out of this world myself." There was some dutiful sniggering and jeers but most eyes were on the skies, watching the dragon's feud unfold. Malath turned slowly back to face Aldrick, a deathly smirk painted on his face. Suddenly, Aldrick felt very small. Malath had a strikingly sinister presence. He was evil, deeply hate-filled.

Aldrick attempted to stow his nerves. "I haven't come so you can see me out of this world, Malath. I am here to avenge my parents. It is your life that will be taken... by me."

"Oh," said Malath contemptuously. "Oh I see. You are trying to be the hero, just as they did." He scowled. "I killed both of them! Your father I turned to ashes on this very ground. And your mother... we found her in her little valley hideaway. My faithful held her down and I slit her throat. Slowly." His deathly expression became one of contemplation. "You must have been nearby that day... a discarded infant."

Rage seared through Aldrick like wildfire. Once more the urge to strike was near overwhelming. He looked across at Jon. Jon looked back with an expression that told he was ready for conflict. His frail fists were clenched.

"Tell me, how it that you come to be here today?" Malath asked. "That dragon—you found it somewhere? That accursed stone was a part of it, wasn't it?" He crossed his arms and chuckled. "Please tell me you weren't planning to try what your mother did. You have not the will to take my storm from me."

"Yes, I found the dragon and yes, the Halfstone was once part of it." Aldrick stood straight. "But I don't think you heard me—I have come for your life. I care not for your storm."

Malath's eyes narrowed. "Oh but you ought to care. The Shard has ascended my power to new heights. You are a pittance before me. I will smite you down!"

Aldrick knew the situation was dire. Just what exactly had he planned to do? He was an ant and Malath was a very large boot. He looked up. Illumir and his adversary circled each other cagily. Their dispute had not yet become violent. He doubted it would be so for much longer.

As if he had somehow sensed the imminent peril below, Illumir suddenly dived and landed again on the court. The dragon rounded on Malath. "You—do you truly intend to battle my friend whilst you possess such deviant power? You must be foul indeed."

"Silence, lizard!" retorted Malath. "With or without the Shard I could snap this whelp in two."

"Is that so? Then why don't you prove it?" Illumir opened his jaws.

Malath reeled back and grasped a pouch that was attached to his belt.

"No!" he cried. "Aashkara, stop this!"

The great red dragon was already in a dive. She swooped down on Illumir and lunged for his neck. Illumir was quick to evade. Suddenly a flickering green object flew from Malath's pouch which the dragon devoured. It was the Shard of Heart's Storm!

"No, NO!" Malath hurled a raging fireball at Illumir. It struck his chest but failed to scorch his stone exterior. Illumir ignored the attack, for now he was caught in a ferocious clash with Aashkara.

"Brother!" A woman draped in blue scurried up to Malath. It was his sister, Selayna. She was hysteric. "Brother, the Sanswords!"

Malath whirled around and looked across the land toward Galdrem. The dust which the Sanswords had stirred was lifting, revealing that the army had all but disappeared—returned to the Life Afterwards. He let out a cry of anguish. "I cannot sustain their life without the Shard! The dragon robbed me of it!"

A number of Malath's followers were fleeing. They feared his loss of power and control. Their faithfulness was not as strong as he might have hoped! This was the opportunity they needed. The battle ground had been levelled, save for the fact that Malath's power remained unequalled.

Aldrick turned to Télia and Kaal. "Keep your distance, both of you. This will be a clash of storm."

"No, fool, remember Jon's teachings. Wield your weapon and your storm as one." Télia looked at him with an expression of both affection and terror.

Aldrick turned away. He couldn't bear the thought of losing her. "If you are to fight, fight only aeras. Have no quarrel with the wielders. Look out for each other. If you are injured call out to be healed… don't die." He drew his sword and faced Malath. The filth and his sister were still lamenting the losses of the Shard and prized army. Now Aldrick glanced across at Jon.

Calmly, Jon looked back and gave a single, subtle nod. He and his friends were ready.

Aldrick knew that he had little chance of defeating Malath if he held onto the anger which seethed inside him, as much as it might stoke his storm. He closed his eyes and took in a deep breath of the afternoon air. He let all sound fade into the background. The roaring and booming of the dragons became muffled murmurs. He pictured his mother's grave in his mind, felt soft golden grass beneath his feet. The flower he had placed on her headstone was still there, fresh and open. The sun was warm, the breeze, cool. He turned around. She and Gilthred stood together in the middle of that crystal clear tarn. They were beaming at him. He smiled back. That same sense of clarity that he had felt after first finding the grave washed over him. Now his storm truly surged within him. It was strong. He opened his eyes.

"Malath!"

Malath stopped speaking with his sister and slowly twisted to face Aldrick. His dark eyes flashed. He drew his own one-handed blade and gripped his staff in the other.

"Well, Aedimon, what are you waiting for?" he yelled savagely.

Aldrick charged at him. In the same moment Jon and his two friends moved on Selayna and Malath's remaining allies. Aldrick's blade became fire in his hands, its metal white hot. Malath stood fast, inviting him to strike. He swung at him with all his might. Malath crossed sword and staff before him, forging a warding wall. As Aldrick's blade struck it, lightning erupted from the tip and lashed at Malath. There was a succession of bright blue flashes and the wielder's staff disintegrated. He staggered back, shaken.

"Ah, your father's trickery," he spat, hastily recomposing himself. "I might have known!"

Now he attacked. A wall of ice struck Aldrick, throwing him across the court. Its sting was agonizing but his hardened nerves made it tolerable. Almost instinctively, he healed himself and found his feet.

"Strong, aren't you!" exclaimed Malath, advancing on him. "The same cannot be said for your parents. Those two were pitiable. They were nothing without those special little abilities of theirs. Your mother stole my powers from me because she was afraid, as you should be. I am almighty and I will destroy you as I did them!" He hurled a raging fireball at Aldrick, who leapt out of its path in the nick of time.

In the corner of his eye, Aldrick saw Télia and Kaal engaged in combat with enemy aeras. He had to take this fight away from them. He bolted for the temple.

"Where are you going, whelp?" Malath pursued him.

Aldrick felt gravity working against him but persisted forward, determined to keep Malath's attention from the others. He sped through the hall, across dust and ruin. Ahead of him, stairs wound up around an abandoned altar. He scaled them and found himself on a huge terrace that overlooked the chasm. He wheeled around. Malath appeared.

"Nowhere to hide now, is there?" he snarled.

Aldrick raised his sword. "Come on!"

Malath lunged at him. Their swords met and fire erupted between them. Malath's fury was fierce, his storm potent. The flames edged closer to Aldrick, licking at his cloak.

Suddenly Malath leapt back. "What... what is this? You're trying your mother's trick now, aren't you?! Do you not think that is cheating, whelp?"

Aldrick realised he had briefly drained some of Malath's storm. Now he felt weak. Wielding the ability had depleted his own.

"It wasn't cheating," he said. "If so, only as much as bringing things back from the dead is."

Malath snorted. "It is my right to do so. I am divinity, with or without the power of the Shard. You on the other hand... you are lesser. You cower behind power that you are unworthy of!" There was a tone of anger in his voice now.

"Tell me then—who is worthy?"

"Those who look up to me."

"You're mad."

"I beg to differ." Malath swung at him. Aldrick lifted his sword in defence but this time it was struck from his hand. A searing pain shot up his arm and he dropped to his knees.

Malath lifted Aldrick's chin with the tip of his blade and leered down at him with hateful eyes. "Time to leave this world, whelp. Die knowing that I will go on and slaughter all whom you hold dear. Then, I will return them and do it again, over and over. I will toy with their souls until they have nothing left, in this world or the next. Your helpless soul will know only of their suffering."

Aldrick felt feeble… empty. There was nothing left to do now. This was the end.

There was a roaring. The figures of the two dragons hurtled past and then came a thunderous crash from below. The floor shuddered and pillars swayed. They must have struck the foundations of the terrace.

"Dear me," remarked Malath, looking around. "Perhaps this temple will be destroyed after all."

Aldrick looked up at him. "You do know what will happen if it is, don't you? That dragon's kin will be freed and the whole world will burn. You won't be divinity for long."

Malath chuckled. "Did the white one tell you this? He too is misguided, then. The banishing is a myth, an old wife's tale—folly rubbish."

"You're wrong."

Malath frowned momentarily, then shook his head. "No, no I am not."

Télia appeared at the top of the stairs. The second Aldrick glanced at her he knew he had made a mistake. Malath noticed his eyes shift and turned.

"What have we here?" he asked gleefully. He looked back at Aldrick, then to her again. "Oh, please tell me this is not your woman…." He laughed. "She is!"

Aldrick panicked. "Télia!"

Malath went for her. She fired an arrow at him, but to no effect. He brushed it aside before grabbing her by the collar and striking her hard across the face.

"Malath." Aldrick forced himself to his feet. "Let her go."

Malath shook his head. "No. Her, you will witness perish before you die."

Aldrick tried to move but found an unyielding warding wall keeping him at bay. Malath strode to the edge of the terrace and held Télia out over the chasm. She didn't struggle. She looked at Aldrick with an expression he could not read.

"Malath... Malath, don't," he pleaded.

Malath's lip curled. "Oh how it must hurt knowing you can do noth—"

In a flash, Télia drew a hidden dagger and drove it into Malath's shoulder. He cried out in pain and let her go. Aldrick watched in horror as she fell from sight.

"No!" He launched himself forward. The warding wall had crumbled. He felt his storm surging from the depths of him. He had power and he had purpose. He drove into Malath with all his might and they both toppled over the edge.

They were falling. Wind beat against them. Below, Télia disappeared into a murky haze. He had to save her but knew Malath would impede him.

"Illumir, catch her!" he yelled out, praying the dragon was near enough to hear him.

Malath let out a merciless laugh. "She is damned."

Aldrick hurled a spear of lightning at him. He deflected it with a shield of fire.

They fought as wrathful beasts, slashing and hammering each other with every element in their control; a battle to honour this gamble of the fates.

Illumir appeared, descending in a dive with Aashkara on his tail. For a moment the dragons fought alongside them, locked in an equally ferocious battle until Illumir broke free and continued down at fierce speed.

"Save her!" Aldrick shouted after him. "Save her!"

Malath dealt a blow that snapped his bones. His sword was lost. He clasped his ribs, healed, then struck back with talons of lightning and shards of ice. Malath blocked.

"Nothing will hinder me!" he cried madly.

Aldrick looked back down to see the haze had thinned and a jagged terrain of scolded stone was rapidly approaching. He held a hand down and tried to slow his descent with gravity. It was hard to focus. He hit the ground at great speed. Malath landed lightly nearby. Dazed and aching, Aldrick lifted his head. Illumir and Aashkara were battling a short distance away from them. Illumir held Télia in his claws. The dragon had caught her! She was alive! He made to find his feet but Malath struck him with earth-shattering force and he hurtled sideways into rock. He collapsed, barely conscious...

He would not give in! Aldrick leapt up and unleashed a blaze upon Malath, who forged a wall, but the flames pushed through. Malath's robes caught alight for an instant before he doused them and retaliated with spears of ice. One pierced Aldrick's chest, slicing like glass. He pulled it out and threw it back. It met Malath's thigh. He grimaced and dropped to one knee. Aldrick saw that he was finding it difficult to heal now. His storm was near spent. So was Aldrick's own. Blood dripped from his chest wound. He staggered forward. Malath gritted his teeth and readied for more.

There was a roar. They both looked sideways. Illumir had his jaws closed around Aashkara's neck. Her talons were lodged deep in his side. With vicious ferocity, Illumir tore her neck wide open. Burning blood gushed to the ground. She grumbled and sputtered then fell sideways, tearing Illumir open as her final act. The dragon toppled over. As he did, his claws opened and Télia jumped to safety. She stood and brushed herself off, then looked up.

"Aldrick!" She ran frantically toward him.

Aldrick looked up. Ruins of the terrace were falling straight for them. Télia launched herself into him and wrapped her body around his. With one hand he held her and with the other he forged a warding wall above them. Malath did the same. The rubble crashed down upon them. Its weight was immense. Aldrick could not withstand it, yet somehow he could. Télia gave him strength. He could not let her die. She would not!

They were smothered in total darkness. The air was choking. "Hold on!"

"I will, Aldrick," she whispered.

From somewhere close, Malath spoke.

"How are you holding up, Aedimon?" he asked. His voice wavered. He was almost done. It was a test of will now.

"Could... be... better," Aldrick replied.

"I... cannot. It... how can this be?" Malath winced.

"How can you…" There was a crumbling sound and then silence. He was dead.

Aldrick held on to Télia and let out a roar. The stone suddenly gave way above them and they ascended, his storm birthing wings beneath them. Télia lifted her head and looked into his eyes. He looked back, feeling devastating exhaustion but overwhelming love.

And so their lips met. They rose higher and higher in gentle embrace and for a time the world around them disappeared.

In the back of his mind, Aldrick heard beating wings. He opened his eyes. Illumir flew past them.

"Thanks for not checking on me," the dragon grumbled in jest. "You are lucky you have your own way back up."

He was thankful to see the dragon alive.

"See you at the top," he called, then continued kissing his future wife.

19

GALDREM

The cool stone floor of Darkna was welcoming. Both ends of the hall were now levelled. The wilting sun's light spilt in, turning rubble to a tender shade of orange. Somewhere, a fantail was chirping happily. Aldrick and Télia collapsed in each other's arms upon landing and for a moment just lay there, taking deep breaths of the still air. The dust had settled.

As Aldrick's thoughts fell upon the others, they came running.

"Aldrick!" Jon cried. "Aldrick, you are alive."

He and Télia stood.

"Yes, we're still here," he said. "As are you."

Jon sighed heavily. "Yes. Malath's followers who remained are no more. Selayna we fought at length, until finally, well, she just shrieked and dropped dead. That was when I presumed Malath had fallen."

Aldrick nodded. "Malath is dead."

Quite out of character, Kaal came and took Aldrick and Télia in his arms. He looked to be unharmed.

"Tell me—is it over, Brother?" he asked, not hiding his weariness.

Aldrick closed his eyes. "I think so."

One of Jon's elderly friends stepped forward. "That dragon of yours—is it friend or foe?"

Aldrick looked to where Illumir awaited on the court. "He is friend to us all. We owe him much."

"Ignoring where you found him, I am curious as to why he had quarrel with Aashkara," said Jon with a furrowed brow. "What were the dragons' motives to involve themselves in this debacle?"

Aldrick now glanced around the crippled temple. "You will know soon."

With Télia's hand in his, Aldrick made his way through the hall to Illumir. The others followed nervously. Doubt was dulling his relief. Was this day truly a victory?

"Hello Aldrick, wielders and humans," Illumir said, meeting them with attentive eyes. "You have questions for me?"

"Yes," Aldrick said, "but first I thank you, Illumir. You saved Télia's life."

"Yes—thank you, Illumir" restated Télia, stepping forward. "I am indebted to you."

Illumir looked upon her kindly. "I did only what I could."

Aldrick surveyed the dragon. "How are you holding up? You were wounded…"

Illumir snorted. "I am quite well. My opponent may

have been large but, in the end, she could not match my stormpower. She spent hers in fire, whereas I restored my body to health."

"What of the Shard's storm?" asked Jon, gazing upon Illumir in wonder. "Do you possess it now?"

"I do. Its power is reserved in me until the day when I must contest with a greater evil."

"Illumir, is that greater evil still at bay?" Aldrick asked nervously.

Illumir surveyed the crippled temple and grumbled. "The seal yet holds, but it has been weakened. Much of the king's storm has left these walls. We must hope he will respond accordingly."

Aldrick's head dropped. So, it was both good news and bad.

Télia stroked his arm.

"Cheer up, gloomy," she said. "This day is a victory."

He managed a grin and leaned in to kiss her.

Kaal groaned and looked away. "Come on, you two. There is a time and a place for that kind of thing."

Jon was scratching his beard. "Can this really be? The Banishing…"

"Indeed, wielder," said Illumir. "It has been a well-veiled truth for ages among your folk."

"Devéna, tell me you knew nothing of this," Jon said, turning to her.

She shook her head. "Honestly, I did not. It would seem that even the highest of the Synod were ignorant of this truth. I assume no one was ever meant to know."

"Correct," affirmed Illumir. "A day such as this may long since have passed, had it been discovered." The dragon looked over each one of them. "You are humble creatures, the lot of you," he said. "Always astonished by what you do not know." He turned and gazed out toward the distant eastern ocean. "There are things I could tell you that would cause the very fabric of your reality to unravel around you. You might find that some things are best left unknown. After all, to wonder can be a greater thing than to know, can it not?"

There was a lengthy silence. Internally, they contemplated much. The day was indeed a victory, Aldrick decided. Télia was in his arms. His mother and father were avenged and the peoples of the land were safe from harm, at least for the time being.

Eventually Jon suggested they all return to Galdrem. Aldrick had looked upon the city from Illumir's back and could see it in the distance now. He was eager to walk within its walls.

Before they left, he went to Illumir's side.

"What will you do now?" he asked.

Illumir surveyed him a moment. "I am undecided, young Aldrick. It has been some time since I last left my hollow. In truth, I find your company agreeable…"

"Well, you are welcome to stay with us for as long as you wish," Aldrick said gladly. "We really must thank you for all this somehow."

The dragon chuckled. "Have a feast in my name, Aldrick." He outstretched his wings. "Do you wish for me to fly you to the gate of the city? Darkness will soon fall."

Aldrick shook his head. "No thanks. A walk in fresh air will do me some good." In truth, he just wanted more time to hold Télia's hand.

"Very well. We shall see each other tomorrow then. I seek not to panic the inhabitants of Galdrem tonight." Illumir launched into the air and flew silently away toward the mountains.

"Good evening, Illumir!" Télia called out after him.

For a while they watched the majestic dragon go, then turned and began to walk down the steps of the temple together, hand in hand.

They met Sinin at the gate of Galdrem. He was with his wife and child, overseeing the last of the citizens' safe return home after fleeing earlier in the day. He was overwhelmed at the sight of them and welcomed them with long and hearty embraces. There were tears of joy in his weary eyes. His family and home might well have been lost to him this day, had fate not shown kindness. Such kindness had not been shown to all, though. Amidst celebration, they found sadness and dismay within the city walls. Scores of the city guard and young scholars of Delthendra had been lost. The highly respected Synod—that which Devéna and Frade belonged to—was all but decimated. Malath had wounded the city deeply and much time would be needed for healing.

Jon was quickly whisked away with Devéna and Frade to an urgent council meeting to discuss the events at Darkna and the revelation that the fabled Banishing was a very real historical event. Aldrick, Télia and Kaal remained with Sinin and his family. After a generous meal in their humble home, Sinin left with Kaal to unwind at a local tavern which had been opened for the night. In turn, Aldrick and Télia bid Leanne and young Flynn a goodnight and walked to the aera's residence in the northwest of the city. It was quiet inside—exactly what they wanted.

Télia showed Aldrick to a small room in which she had slept during her training. They collapsed on her bed and, for a long time, just lay in each other's arms. There were so many things to be thinking and reflecting upon, but right now all they cared for was each other. They had earned this time.

Sometime in the early morning, Télia led him to the bathhouse, where they washed away layers of dust and sweat from their bodies. She was careful to have a curtain drawn between them, because she was shy, he assumed. This proved not to be so, as when he returned to her room, he found her unclothed in bed with but a sheet covering her thighs. He tried not to stare. Her beauty was inexpressible. Her long locks fell in damp flurries around her. Her emerald eyes gazed straight into his soul.

"Come here," she said quietly.

He dropped everything and went to her. They began to kiss—gentle pecks. For each one he would have traversed a desert, had he been requested, but here they were wilfully surrendering themselves to each other. Little by little, their kisses became firmer and fiercer as their passion soared. Finally all restraint was lost…

20

BETWEEN THE MOUNTAINS AND THE SEA

For the first time in a week, there was no need to rise early. Aldrick and Télia spent the spare hours snoozing peacefully. Eventually they were woken by one of Télia's good friends who lived in the aera's residence. They ate breakfast with her before returning to Sinin's. Both Kaal and Jon had slept there.

"Ah, you two," remarked Jon upon their arrival. "I had almost begun to worry."

"We needed a good rest."

Sinin winked at them. "It was about time you two had a 'good rest'."

"How did the meeting go last night, Jon?" asked Télia, ignoring Sinin's cheek.

Jon sighed. "Oh, you know politics. There was a lot of shouting and little actual discussion. The council found the whole deal with the dragons difficult to swallow. We did at least manage to convince them that Illumir poses no threat to us."

"I hear the dragon is outside the city wall," said Sinin. "He's been giving farmers and livestock a right scare."

"I think he's waiting for you, Aldrick," prompted Kaal.

Aldrick nodded. "I should go and see him." He turned to Télia. "Will you come?"

"Of course."

As they made their way down the main city street, they noticed numerous people eying them. Some murmured in the ears of those close to them, others pointed. A few cheered. They must have heard details of the battle at Darkna.

Télia nudged him. "All eyes on you, huh?"

"Me? Why me?!"

She grinned. "You're the hero."

He shook his head. "No I'm not. I did no more than anyone else did yesterday, no more than you."

She snorted. "That's the kind of thing a hero would say."

"Is it?"

"Yes." She stopped and looked up at him. "Aldrick, you took on Malath. You saved this city and its people."

"I may have taken him on, but I never defeated him. He was just unlucky."

"Perhaps, yet you survived him all the same. You outlasted him. How many can claim that?"

"And what does that prove? That I'm a lucky fool?"

She wrapped her arms round him. "You're a fool to be sure. But what it proves is that you are courageous and powerful. You are now perhaps the most powerful wielder who lives."

"How much power I have is not something I have any say in."

"Oh look—speaking like a hero again," she said playfully.

He laughed sarcastically and they continued on.

The city gate was opened upon their approach. Beyond, the surrounding farmland was eerily quiet. This was because Illumir had settled himself in a nearby field. The dragon looked to be dozing in the sun. A flock of terrified sheep were huddled in the far corner of the field, adamantly looking in the opposite direction.

As they neared, Illumir unfurled and stretched. "Ah, Aldrick and Télia, I have awaited you."

"Sorry for keeping you."

"It is of no matter." The dragon rose to his feet. "I have enjoyed bathing here in the sun."

Télia lifted her head so that the sun's rays caught her face. "It's lovely, isn't it?"

Illumir looked from her to Aldrick. "I like this one. She feels life, as you do. You will do well together."

"Thanks," Aldrick said awkwardly.

Télia flushed.

"What will you do now, Aldrick? With the foul wielder demised, where will you go from here?"

"Home," he answered. "I may have lost two parents, but I am blessed to have a complete family in this life. I'm looking forward to seeing them again."

"Ah yes." Illumir looked to the sky. "Home is a

good place to be."

Aldrick suddenly felt deep sorrow for the dragon. "You will speak with your king, won't you? He might decide to allow you back. You deserve that."

"No, he will never allow me back. Such a change of heart would be viewed as weakness by our kind. He would not be seen that way." Illumir looked down again.

Télia was watching him. "Maybe up there isn't where you belong, Illumir. Maybe your home is here with us…"

The dragon grumbled broodingly.

"Perhaps you are right, Télia," he said, then turned to Aldrick. "May I take you back to your family? It would be an honour."

"If you can spare the time, that would be greatly appreciated," Aldrick said, pleased that Illumir had offered. He was eager to view the world from the sky once more.

"Well then, let me know when and I shall be waiting for you here in this field."

"At noon tomorrow?" Aldrick suggested. "I want to spend a little more time in Galdrem first."

"At noon," Illumir repeated. "Very well. We will see each other then." He launched into the sky and flew away toward the peaks of the Mountains Nemduran once more.

Aldrick and Télia walked back to the city gate. As it opened, there was a spirited neigh behind them. De'ama, Tame and Stub were galloping down the road toward them. They were a welcome sight. The couple greeted the horses joyfully, then led them to some stables and paid to have them well attended to.

That evening, after a lengthy tour of the sprawling city, they attended a public celebration of peace and a commemoration to those who had lost their lives during Malath's seizure of the city. It took place in the Garden District. Hundreds of small lanterns had been hung from the trees and lit up their surroundings in warm colours. Seats and tables were arranged on the grass underneath them. The tables were laden with sumptuous foods and there was drink on tap.

To Aldrick's bewilderment, he had been allocated a seat at a table with members of the city council and those who remained of the Synod. During speeches, mugs were raised to thank him and the others for standing against peril and adversity. Devéna openly offered him an honorary position in the Synod, which he immediately accepted under pressure. When he was offered the opportunity to speak, he made a point to note Illumir's role as true saviour of the city and lands, for it was he who had stopped the army of Sanswords and he who had defeated Aashkara. To this there was much cheering in Illumir's name and Aldrick was spontaneously dubbed 'Dragon Rider'. He didn't object.

Never was there a mention of the danger which still lurked deep below them. This was a good thing. It was not the time or place to speak of such dark things. Besides, there was no knowing whether those dragons would ever become a threat. Illumir had said the seal still held at Darkna.

Aldrick mused on something else the dragon had said: "To wonder can be a greater thing than to know." Perhaps it was a good thing that one could never know exactly what the future held. Assuming everlasting peace was foolish, and dwelling on doubt was more so. It was this fleeting moment that was to be revelled in and cherished… he finished his pint.

When the hour was late, people began to drunkenly stagger away to their respective dwellings. Some continued on to taverns around the city. Kaal and Sinin were part of the latter group, this time accompanied by Jon and Frade. After reminding Kaal to be ready for the journey home at noon, Aldrick and Télia returned to the aera's residence.

"Do you realise how lucky you are that you dismissed me as your aera?" Télia asked, removing his clothes at her bedside. "This would be so very frowned upon, especially in my room."

"I dismissed you for that exact reason," he joked.

She slapped him. "Idiot."

He took her in his arms. "Will you come with me tomorrow?" he asked hopefully. "Come south with me. Meet my family. Enjoy some quiet time between the mountains and the sea."

She beamed. "I will."

"Good," he said gladly.

They began to kiss and slowly…

A large audience had gathered for their departure even though the weather was sour. Aldrick was uncertain if the crowds had come to farewell them, or to witness the greatness of Illumir. People gazed upon the dragon in marvel. Those who dared not tread too close watched from the heights of the city wall.

Jon was the first to say his goodbyes. He was to remain in Galdrem, to spend time with old friends and oversee the rebuild of Delthendra and the Synod's tower.

"Take care, won't you?" he said, addressing them all. "It will be cold down there very shortly. Wrap up warm and don't hesitate to wander north from time to time."

"Definitely," Aldrick said, embracing him. "In fact, I might come back with Télia in a few weeks to fetch our horses. Whether you are home or still in Galdrem, we will stop by to say hello."

Jon's eyes twinkled.

"Very good," he said. "You will say hello to Braem, Vara and young Bree for me, won't you?"

Aldrick patted him on the back. "I will, Jon." He turned away, then immediately back on his heel. "Jon, how am I here?" he asked. "How did I endure Malath? He was unrelenting. I felt his storm overwhelming mine many times. Still, I breathe... I don't understand."

Jon smiled. "Aldrick..." The old wielder's head drooped and then he looked away into the distance — into some memory of long ago. "I like to believe that the hatred of many can be dissolved by the love for a few," he said wistfully.

Aldrick knew Jon's mind lingered on Isobel and

Gilthred. "Jon, my parents are still here...."

Jon looked back at him with his smile returning. "Yes," he said. "Yes, I do believe they are."

"Did... did they have a sign, like Selayna did?" Aldrick was fairly certain he already knew the answer.

"They did—a black fantail."

At that very moment the friendly fantail appeared, hovered between him and Jon for a moment, then went chirping away and perched on an oblivious Illumir.

"You are in the company of angels, Aldrick," Jon whispered.

Aldrick watched his two winged friends for a time, then looked over at Télia. "Yes, I am."

When all farewells were said and done, he kicked Kaal. "Are you ready, Brother?"

"Am I ever!" Kaal exclaimed, eagerly clambering up onto Illumir's back.

He turned to Télia.

She grinned. "Always."

Aldrick took her hand and they found a seat together between Illumir's spires.

The dragon turned his long neck to look at them.

"Are you ready?" he asked.

"We are."

"Then let us be off. Brace yourselves." Illumir launched his mighty stone body into the air and they began to ascend into the sky.

Aldrick took a breath. He was feeling great now. Everything was great. He felt in touch and at peace with everyone and everything around him. It was a feeling he would bear home with him. His life may have changed drastically since he left their modest farm on the mountainside, but all the same, it was home and always would be.

Looking down, Aldrick saw the crowds waving up at them. As a final gesture of goodwill and farewell he raised his hand and for leagues around them the clouds dispersed, allowing sunlight to flood down upon the land. There was thunderous applause.

Télia squeezed him. "Show-off."

Illumir swooped into a smooth glide and they were on their way.

ABOUT THE AUTHOR

Daniel was raised in a remote mountainous region of the South Island, New Zealand. He lived on a 23-acre lifestyle block of regenerating forest with his parents and three siblings. The beautiful natural scenery and quietness he was surrounded by was the perfect environment for his imagination to run wild with fantasies of what the larger world could be. Around the age of 12, Daniel first envisioned *The Narathlands* — a world full of magic, adventure and mystery. For nearly a decade, this world was little more than a small collection of messily written notes and simple sketches. However, after completing a Bachelor of Arts degree at Victoria University of Wellington, Daniel found time to continue work on a novel set in this world. Over the years his eagerness to do so never waned. This novel is in your hands and a sequel is on the cards.

Facebook:
Daniel White Author